A Sea Glass Christmas

Sea Glass Inn
Book 5

Julie Carobini

DOLPHIN GATE BOOKS

JULIE CAROBINI's inspirational beach romances are known for spunky heroines, charming heroes, quirky friends, and the secrets they keep. Her bestselling titles include *Walking on Sea Glass* and *Runaway Tide,* and she has received awards from The National League of American Pen Women and ACFW. Mom to three grown kids, Julie lives in California with her husband, Dan, and their rescue pup, Dancer. Visit JulieCarobini.com.

For Dan, the hero I always write

Chapter 1

I'll Be Home for Christmas

Trace Murphy glanced around the lobby of the Sea Glass Inn, a tingle running up her spine. Nothing out of place. It was all there—the garland of blue spruce, silver tinsel, twinkling lights, and cheerful music reminding everyone of the joys of Christmas. Like in times past, a bellringer stood outside the lobby doors, collecting change for the less fortunate.

For more than ten years, Trace had worked at the hotel's concierge desk and the traditions from year to year had stayed the same. The pipers were piping, the carolers were caroling, and the duffers were, well, they were still golfing. Even in December along the coast of California.

She waved to a crew of four that wandered through the lobby in their garish outfits after a day out on the course, and by the looks of them, a few beers to celebrate the eighteenth hole.

Her phone trilled. She usually kept it in her purse, but she was waiting for a text from her mother regarding her

1

flight details for Christmas this year. Trace would be picking her up from the airport, so the minute she received that text with the details, she would put a vacation day on the calendar.

But instead of a flight number, she received a notification of another kind: a picture on social media. She enlarged it with a swipe of two fingers. Four women, all co-workers, were having dinner together tonight. Trace scrolled through her mind but couldn't recall hearing a thing about a girls' night out.

She dropped her phone into a drawer and began idly straightening a stack of brochures. If she were honest, it didn't surprise her at all that she hadn't been invited to the gathering. Though she'd been with the inn for more than a decade, she was just an employee, a worker bee who flitted in and out of the confidences of the higher-ups at their whim. Not that she didn't love them all—she did. But sometimes ... well, she almost wondered if anyone would notice if she did something crazy, like take a month off for the Caribbean.

Kidding, of course. Murphy family members were built with a strong work ethic. She would never allow a little thing like a missed dinner party invitation keep her down. And besides, even if she had been invited to their soiree, she couldn't have gone because she was on duty tonight.

Speaking of which, Trace glanced around at the bustling lobby again. Smiling faces everywhere, heels clicking, gift bags rustling, guests in need of dinner recommendations and other advice.

Her eyes locked on a man who had appeared like some

sort of heavenly messenger at the front desk. He exuded an otherworldliness in his form-fitted button-down shirt and inky blue jeans. An angel who worked out, apparently. Alas, she peeled her gaze away. She had work to do! People *needed* her to be on top of everything here at the inn tonight.

"Excuse me? Where's the bathroom?"

Trace flinched. She focused on the teen girl staring back at her, unsmiling, gum snapping. "The bathroom?" the girl repeated.

For what seemed like the thousandth time today, Trace found a smile, then proceeded to politely direct the young guest to the restrooms "down the hall and to the right." She watched the girl get swallowed up in the mad crisscross of lobby guests, twirling her hair and swinging her skinny hips as she did.

Such was life as a concierge for a seaside resort.

Trace took in the lobby again, a little less wonder in her soul. Shouldn't all these people be out Christmas shopping or something? If the holiday romance channel was to be believed, this season was meant for listening to street carolers while browsing craft fairs or traveling to snow-packed, idyllic small towns for days of shushing down the slopes. And gifts. Lots and lots of gifts piled as high as all that snow.

"Hey, fart face," Thomas cackled.

Trace frowned. She swung a look over at the valet who had made it his mission to annoy her. The angelic man checking in at the front desk must have heard him too because he looked over his shoulder at her. Trace's face burned and she refocused on Thomas. "What do you want?"

"To be able to grow a mustache like yours."

She slapped her hand across her upper lip. She'd been bleaching that thing since her teen years, never suspecting that anyone noticed it but her. Naturally, Trace had always blamed her mother for this. *Thanks a lot, Mom, for passing that attribute down to me.*

My goodness, that's what wax is for! Her mother always said. *Remember—no pain, no gain, sweet cheeks.*

Trace glared at Thomas. "Maybe when you hit puberty, you'll get what's coming to you."

He jogged away, wiggling his hand in the air, as if weighing her response.

So. It was going to be one of those nights. Well, she *had* drawn the short straw when she found herself working the concierge desk this evening. She still didn't know exactly how that happened but had a guess. Nobody wanted the shift, and the higher-ups said, "No big deal—Trace'll do it."

They were right, of course, but a needling inside of her wondered if she ought to start thinking about a future that didn't include working for a team that took her presence for granted—including a valet who was beginning to cross the line with his so-called "friendly" teasing.

Problem was, she loved the inn, and it would be hard to say goodbye. Very hard. She never would.

Would she?

A sudden part in the sea of tourists gave Trace another view of the front desk. That heavenly being at check-in was tucking something—a room key, maybe?—into the back pocket of his jeans. His Levi's sat low on his hips, clinging to him like a low-slung tool belt, and could she help it if she needed a little visual respite from the frenetic activity of the hotel lobby tonight?

Her desk phone trilled. "Concierge desk, Trace speaking."

"Hey, Trace, it's Gil." Gil managed tee times at the golf club nearby. "Sun's out tomorrow so we're expecting a crowd. Got your list for me?"

"Yes, of course." Quickly, Trace ran her gaze down the list on her desk, reviewing the golf roster. "Tell you what, Gil. I'd feel better if I went online to the portal to make sure every one of our sign-ups has a confirmed time. Okay if I do that and confirm via email?"

"Sure thing."

She logged in, opened the portal, and compared the list, line by line. Success. Every guest had a nice juicy slot on the fairway tomorrow. She should have exited out, but temptation snared her like a second slice of pumpkin pie after Thanksgiving dinner.

She clicked back over to the post she'd stumbled on earlier. Below the selfie of Liddy, Meg, Sophia, and Priscilla—four inn staff members—was the caption: *Having a fabulous time!*

She clicked away. Wouldn't want anyone to call her a voyeur or anything. But that tiny niggling from earlier in the evening began to gnaw a little deeper. She was happy for them, really. All work and no play wasn't a saying for nothin'.

But ... when was the last time they had asked her to join them?

Finally, the mystery man turned away from the front

desk, giving her a better view. He pulled a suitcase behind him and headed toward the bank of elevators—alone. *Would you look at that?* Surely he had a gorgeous wife or girlfriend around the corner. Trace rubbernecked a look toward the inn's glass entry doors. She expected to see a woman with a mane of hair that didn't need extensions to look amazing stroll in. The woman would slip her arm into the crook of his and disappear with him into the sunset, *er,* elevator.

So far, no one. The lobby reverberated with Kelly Clarkson singing "Please Come Home for Christmas." Kind of appropriate for a guy away from home during the holidays.

And a girl who couldn't remember the last time she'd spent the holiday with loved ones, other than her cat.

What was wrong with her? This was not a time for the spirit of bah-humbug to raise its pointy little head. Christmas was around the bend, as was a very big birthday for her. Every year, she shared her day with the Lord and never resented it. True, this one was a milestone of sorts. She didn't care to think too much about that, though.

The view through westward-facing windows showed that the sun was about to set. Soon an automatic timer would light up the giant Christmas tree in the lobby for the night and the toy train that sped around it once an hour would begin its noisy trip.

Trace clucked her tongue at the thought. Liddy, the hotel's PR manager and Trace's former concierge co-worker, had insisted on adding the train. And for the first, oh, six or seven times around the track, Trace enjoyed its rumble and whistle. But by the twentieth or so time, she put up a bit of a fuss.

"The next time I hear that train, I'm going to wring its neck!" she had told the inn's VP, Meg Riley. Meg stuck a fist into her hip. "I don't think that's possible, Trace."

"All I'm saying is the Southern Pacific Railroad over there was a nice idea, but I'm about to fill it with coal. It's driving me crazy."

Liddy had pulled up to the desk about then, concern on her face. "Hm. I think we can set it to go around the track fewer times. Say, six times an hour?"

Trace cocked her head. "How about once?"

Liddy gasped, but Meg nodded her head in that succinct way of hers. "I like that. It'll be something everyone will look forward to on the hour." She looked across the lobby then and spotted Hans, the front desk manager. He had been with the hotel almost as long as Trace, only his face was the one that typically wore the scowl.

"Hans," Meg said, "have one of the bellmen reset the train, please. I'd like it to run at the top of the hour only."

He gave her a salute and that was that. Trace tensed up every hour on the hour since.

Hannah appeared next to Trace, causing her to jerk her chin up. "You look like you could use a break," Hannah said. She stepped behind the circular desk, ready to stand in while Trace took a break.

"Thanks," Trace said. "I brought some food, so I'll just get my bag."

"You know, you could always eat down in the galley."

That was the euphemism they all used for the windowless employee lounge downstairs.

"And lose my lunch? No, thanks."

Hannah rolled her eyes. "While it's true that the new chef is nowhere near as good as Chef Franco was, I think you'd be pleasantly surprised anyway."

Trace shrugged. It was generous of Riley Holdings, the inn's owner, to provide meals for staff, leftovers from various hotel functions—reimagined, of course—but she didn't have any interest in consuming even one more bite of Chicken à la King or rewarmed steak over rice. She looped an insulated bag over her shoulder and tucked a novel under her arm. "I'm good. Thanks."

"Okay," Hannah said, "enjoy your celery and peanut butter dinner."

Trace pivoted. "That was one time! Besides, peanut butter and celery is healthy—and a staple." She could hear Hannah's laughter even as she made her way down the hall where she exited to the grassy area overlooking the water.

Though the sun was ready to set, Trace wasn't cold. How weird was that? Mid-December and still able to sit outside. At least for a while. She fished a peanut butter and jelly sandwich out of her bag, but before she could take a bite, a text pinged her phone. It was from her mother.

Sorry, kiddo. I won't be able to make it for Christmas this year after all.

And just like that, her appetite disappeared. Trace re-read the text. Pretty matter of fact and she almost wondered if her mother was relieved. Dinah Murphy left California for Florida several years ago and never looked back. She knew, though, how tough it would be for Trace to leave the hotel during the holidays, so she promised to visit for Christmas.

Only she never had.

Trace stuffed her dinner back into the bag and watched that giant ball of fire drop into the distant horizon, taking her oomph with it. Another day done. A flutter of emotion tickled her throat but she wouldn't give in to it. So her mother couldn't make it for Christmas? She'd survive.

Behind her, the new chapel stood watch, and for some reason, just knowing that brought her comfort. Trace had worked at the inn long enough to remember when the land that the chapel sat on was an unused portion of turf. And now it stood, a stalwart, both strong and inviting.

The chapel wasn't actually new any longer, though it still felt that way to her. In reality, the cozy building had already hosted hundreds of weddings, including both Sophie's—she co-owned the inn with her brother, Jackson Riley—and Priscilla's to that hunky billionaire she snagged.

Trace leaned in toward the steepled building and frowned. Why was the light on? Nothing was scheduled to happen in the chapel tonight. Of all people, she would know.

A tingly sensation skittered along her arm. She'd told anyone and everyone who would listen that the inn had been the victim of theft lately. Housekeeping had been reporting an uptick in missing towels, monogrammed robes, and other decorative items from rooms, but would anyone listen? Not really. Who'd want to steal a thermostat cover with SGI on it anyway? Her reports were met with shrugs.

Trace closed her eyes. Maybe a vacation was in order. Yes, that was it. She would plan something for January when the inn was less busy, maybe even to Florida. The thought calmed her some, and she let the night's cool sea air wash over her face. When she opened her eyes again, the nagging began anew. She zeroed in on the chapel's illuminated windows.

If her cat, Agatha, were with her, she might slink herself right inside to make sure that all was well. Maybe she would emerge with a mouse in her jaws, a big red bow tied around its neck.

She should leave well enough alone. It wasn't her job to chase after every question like it was a clue to some giant mystery. Then again, it was Christmas. Where was her holly jolly? Her jingle jangle?

With a groan and acceptance that her curiosity could not be contained, Trace tiptoed over and peeked through the window. Nothing but pews awash in light from chandeliers above, their silvery wood looking warm, inviting.

She stepped inside, memories flooding her. The inn changed after this chapel was added. Locals who'd never stepped inside the resort wandered in for quiet moments and brides put it on their short lists because ... how many inns had a chapel? She remembered the pride she'd felt when Jackson, along with his wife, Meg—who had worked at the inn for years—announced what would be built on this patch of lawn at the top of the cliff.

Trace wandered down the center aisle, breathing in the scent of pine—the real stuff coming from the scraggly tree a couple of bellmen dragged in here a week ago, not the fake spray kind (though she wasn't averse to dousing her apartment with it when the mood struck).

She settled onto a pew and took a deep breath. This is what she needed. To center herself. To rest. To think about her blessings instead of grousing about the annoyances that needled her. She was on display in her job, eight hours a day of being "on," of multitasking to give every guest the sense that they were the only person who mattered.

It was important. It was also exhausting. Trace exhaled. Self-help wasn't really her thing. Her mom had avoided that sort of introspection, too. "We're made of sturdier stuff," she'd say.

But ... taking this few minutes now for herself helped her to realize how much she needed the quiet. No wonder the hotel spa was so popular. She was too cheap to spend that kind of money on creams and potions, but she had to admit, some of those wrinkled old ladies came out looking ten years younger. Or at least five.

Might be something to that.

Eyes closed now, she drew in another deep breath and began to feel her body melting into the pew. This kind of relaxation came totally free, and she was all about that.

Someone behind her cleared his throat and said, "Hello." A male voice.

Trace jerked her chin in the voice's direction. "Ouch!" Her neck spasmed from the sudden movement.

The man standing over her cocked an eyebrow. She lowered both of her own brows, trying to control the naturally occurring glower in her gaze.

It was ... him.

She swallowed, finding her voice again. "Can I help you?"

"No, thanks." He glanced at the novel she'd dropped onto the pew. The cover model had, apparently, forgotten to wear a shirt. He snapped another look at her face, a tease of a smile on his mug.

Great. It wasn't even her book—her co-worker, Stephanie, had left it behind and she'd grabbed it without looking at the cover. Not that this was *any* of his business.

She tossed her lunch bag over the novel as he walked past her, then slowed to stand in front of one of the chapel's uniquely shaped windows.

Well, this was something. He was looking all sexy holding a measuring tape, his jeans-clad hip leaning on a pew. Ought to be outlawed to look like that in a chapel. She was old-fashioned that way.

He turned a look over his shoulder, as if wondering if she was still there and watching him from behind. Heat and sweat surged across her skin. "You sure I can't help you with something?"

"I am." He shoved off the pew. "Sorry to have bothered your ... quiet time." He gestured toward one of the diamond-shaped stained-glass windows. "Just need a few measurements and then I'll be out of your way."

You're not in my way, dreamboat ... stud ... Fabio-wannabe ...

Her mind raced. She didn't have any experience with flirtatious banter, but if she did, she'd be laying some of that on him right now.

"Measurements, huh?"

He quirked a sideways grin at her.

Wait. Did she just say something ... suggestive? Gah. She was not any good at this at all.

"Yes," he said. "My client has admired these windows for some time. I'm here to collect some, um, specs."

"They are beautiful—my favorite part of this chapel, though I love the whole place. Who knew windows could take that shape?"

"Whoever created them is an artist."

"Mm-hm."

He chuckled. "With the right tools, I could slip them right out of their frames."

She froze. "You're saying you would *steal* the windows?"

His eyes widened. "Of-of course not." His chuckle faded away.

"So ... you're measuring them ... for a client."

He looked away quickly, all business now. "Yep."

Hm.

Loretta, their housekeeping supervisor, mentioned again this morning that more towels than usual had been missing. When Trace pressed her, she added, "And a few irons."

Again, neither Meg nor Jackson seemed all that concerned, as if this was the price of doing business.

She turned again to the man with the tape measure. Could he have been casing the place?

The man's back was to her now. His muscular arms stretched toward the ceiling, the measuring tape telescoped upward. Not exactly a train wreck, but seriously, how could she look away from this spectacle?

Well. The man might have sympathetic Ryan eyes—

that's what she called crystal blue eyes that reminded her of Ryan Gosling's in "The Notebook," not to mention a strong chin and the kind of luxurious hair that some woman—not her, of course—might want to run their fingers through.

But that didn't mean he couldn't possibly be up to no good. Experience had taught her that sometimes people let you down. Even the ones you never thought would. Maybe even the handsome stranger who had minutes ago checked into the Florence suite. (She might have checked the inn's guest list ...)

He turned. Lifted the measuring tape. "Got what I needed."

"So this boss of yours," she said, "is he doing some redecorating at home?"

The man frowned. He scrunched those eyebrows together. If she were to reach up, she could massage away his confusion with her light touch ... Stop that!

When he didn't answer her, she blurted out, "May I suggest a Pottery Barn catalog instead?'

He lifted a brow. "They don't sell windows like this in Pottery Barn." He paused. "Ma'am."

He did not just call her *ma'am.*

The Greek god, er, hotel guest stepped toward her, that spot between his eyes dipping slightly. She was trying very hard not to stare at it ...

"I was kidding about the windows," he said, catching eyes with her. "Trace, is it?"

She nodded.

"You're pretty protective of this place. Does it—"

A gruff voice interrupted him. "Oh. You got in. Good."

The rotund man standing in the doorway held up a wad of keys. "They told me at the front desk you needed to get in, but you beat me to it." He glanced at Trace and narrowed his eyes, like he was thinking. "Or maybe, uh, she let you in?"

Trace frowned. "You seriously don't know my name, Otis?"

He pressed his mouth together until the proverbial light went on in his eyes. "Right. It's Tracy. Forgot that."

She shook her head and through gritted teeth said, "It's Trace. No 'y'."

Otis pursed his lips. "Kind of odd, isn't it?"

The jeans-clad man, the one suddenly in an awkward position, stuck out his hand to her. "Trace, I'm Noah."

She laughed. He was kidding, right?

He gave her a look that said, *Did I say something wrong?*

Well, of course, his name was Noah. He didn't just resemble Ryan Gosling, he shared the same name as his iconic hero in "The Notebook."

She could not have planned this better herself.

"If we're done here," Otis said, interrupting her musing, "I'll get back to it."

"Otis?" Trace was looking toward the grand, double-door entry now. On one side, a lighted sconce illuminated the chapel. But on the other, the light was not only out—it was missing.

She continued, "Did you remove that sconce?"

Otis frowned and stepped quickly over to the wall beside the door. Nothing but a hole with some wires sticking out of it. He scratched his significantly round head. "Nobody told me they were gonna change this light out."

"So it's just gone?"

"Would seem so." He pulled out a small notepad and pen and began scribbling on it. "I'll check the bucket for a work order on this. Don't remember seein' one."

After Otis left, the silence crackled between Trace and Noah. He was watching her. "Like I was saying earlier, you seem protective of the inn."

"And you think that's odd?"

"Not in the least. I think it's charming." He shifted his hip, leaning up against a pew again. She tried not to let her gaze linger on that small action. "If more people cared about what was happening around them, the world would be a kinder place."

For once, Trace didn't have a quip to lob back. She didn't have much to add to that at all, because, quite frankly, she felt the same way.

Noah stuck the measuring tape in his back pocket. "It's been a pleasure meeting you, Trace. I'll be here for the next three weeks, so I'll see you around."

She opened her mouth to reply, but her tongue couldn't keep up. Instead of saying, *Yes, you too. It's been a pleasure*, the only thing she said was, "Yoop."

Chapter 2

It's Beginning to Look a Lot Like Christmas

For a project of this size, Noah could have sent one of his guys. Normally, that's exactly what he would have done. But the idea of spending another Christmas alone wasn't all that appealing to him. Even introverts needed to see people on occasion, especially during the holidays.

He kicked off his boots and leaned into the couch, taking in the chandelier above. This suite was too grand for him, but he liked it. Italian-inspired furnishings—a suede couch and two leather wingback chairs. Hadn't expected that at a beachside inn.

He leaned forward, resting his elbows on his knees. As he thought more about it, this was the reason his client hired him to bird dog the artistic touches on this property, wasn't it? Because of the attention to detail? The same kinds of touches his client hoped to emulate.

Noah slapped his palms onto his thighs, got up, and wandered into the kitchenette. Open shelving. Colorful plates, mugs—and a Moka Pot. Whoa. He searched further. Yep. Robust, dark coffee and a grinder tucked into the corner beneath richly colored tile.

From what he'd heard, one of the owners of Sea Glass Inn was not only Italian by birth, she had lived in Italy much of her life, so she had inspired some changes to the place. He chuckled, taking it all in. "Well, then. Buon Natale to me."

His smile dulled. Why did the thought of a beachside Christmas bring on a wave of melancholy?

Plenty of people spent their holidays in a hotel. There were movies made about faraway travel during the holidays. And while he might not have planned this, interjecting himself into this overwhelming project had been perfect timing. Sure, he could have joined his parents in Maine, but all that snow?

No, thank you.

Ten years ago, his parents started their yearly tradition of spending Christmas in the coldest weather they could think of. He shook his head, trying to wrap his brain around that all these years later. His mom and dad opted to fly north every winter, while every other person of means in their age group did the exact opposite.

"Chopping wood keeps me young," his father always proclaimed. Noah had believed him at first, until he caught his mother giggling into her hand. She finally admitted that they had a season's worth of firewood delivered at the first sign of moisture in the air.

Ha. No way did he need that this year.

He fished his leftover lunch out of the fridge, dumped the pasta dish into a bowl, and popped it into the microwave. Who was he kidding? There was more to Noah's reticence in joining his parents for Christmas. It came down to ... too much pressure.

Even in the dead of winter, they would find a single woman to fix him up with. Happened every year. Every. Year. No amount of begging (or threatening) had kept his mother from whipping out a tattered photo from his college years and thrusting it in front of some unsuspecting woman out for a day of Christmas shopping. He cringed thinking of the poor women stuck in lines, unable to escape his mother's savvy way with a segue.

"My, that's a beautiful sweater!"

"Who does your hair, darlin'? It's lovely!"

"Are you available to date my well-employed son?"

"And will you give me three grandchildren or four?"

He clucked his tongue. Who needed online dating when Brenda Bridges was on the job?

Something in his gut twisted. His mother never gave up, even when her meddling went very wrong. He fought back a curse just thinking about it. And in some weird and wretched way, he still held out hope that ...

No. He raked a hand through his hair and idly looked at his dinner spinning in that microwave. He didn't want to hold out hope that last year's torment could somehow turn around this season. Unfortunately, the thought was still there, needling him.

Shew. He wasn't all that hungry, but the smell of pasta warming helped. A little, anyway. It had been a long day, and he knew how he got if he didn't eat—irascible as a grumpy old man waiting for a table. He grabbed the remote on the counter and pointed it toward the television in the kitchen. One of two in the suite—though the other was much larger. He began scrolling through the offerings. News, food shows, and documentaries about sea life.

Meh.

His mind drifted to the spunky woman he'd met in the chapel. Eyes of fire, that one. She questioned him like she owned the resort, rather than worked there. He bit the fleshy underside of his bottom lip. His presence seemed to perturb her. Why did that bug him?

Maybe he had just interrupted her solitude when he wandered inside the quiet little place with work on his mind. That was probably it. Nobody liked to have their peace taken from them, especially when those moments were few and far between. The inn had been a madhouse when he wandered in after an eight-hour-plus drive from Arizona. And that dude that parked cars—even he wanted to pummel him for the way he spoke to her.

No wonder she'd seemed testy. He didn't blame her for wanting some quiet time.

Or maybe ... he cringed. Shouldn't have made that stupid quip about stealing windows. That seemed to turn their conversation away from pleasantries to something that simmered inside of her. Unlike his mother, he wasn't all that great with the segue. More than once he'd tried out internet dating, and more than once, women would tell him he was a mystery, then give him their excuse for not accepting a second date.

"I'm too young for commitment."

"You're too ... old for me."

"I don't date guys in construction."

Noah grunted a sigh. None of them would live up to

the relationship he'd had, well, the one he *thought* was a match. He'd avoided his mother for weeks after that, imagining how their conversation would go.

"She was *perfect* for you, son."

"Is it possible," he would ask her, "that she was actually perfect for *you?*"

His mother would dab at her tears. "Isn't that the same thing?"

He groaned, not wanting to think about it. Mainly because a sinking sensation in his insides told him he wouldn't find anything like that again for a long, long time.

The microwave dinged, telling him that dinner was ready.

Noah didn't need anything else to go wrong on this project. Already the bank was threatening liquid damages if they didn't hit pre-set milestones by the end of the year. No. Having the staff at this resort eyeing him suspiciously wouldn't work for him.

Plate in hand, he collapsed back onto the couch and rubbed his neck with a rough palm, massaging out the knots that had formed overnight. He set his plate on the coffee table. Maybe he would drop a peace offering off at the concierge desk on his way to tomorrow's meeting with his client. That ought to smooth things over with the woman who had eyed him with such suspicion, right?

He cracked a wry smile. His mother would be so proud.

"Agatha, what's wrong with me?" Trace took a long sip of her energy smoothie and plunked her cup on the table as if she'd just sidled up to a barkeep. "Don't look at me like that. I need some serious advice here, and you're about the only one in my life right now who seems to care."

Her cat stared her down, like she had a point to make.

"You're saying that I need to check my attitude, aren't you?" Trace looked out the window where her neighbor, Jan, had just tossed a wetsuit over the railing. She swung a look back to Agatha. "You might be right. Maybe I did jump to some conclusions last night."

Agatha let out a low meow, the kind that expressed disappointment. She did it again.

"Paranoid is a strong word, but I see what you're saying. Not sure what's going on with me, but I've been off my game lately." Trace sighed at a rush of thoughts. "Noah —that's his name—*is* going to be staying at the inn for three weeks. How will I survive seeing all that hunkiness walking around in front of me? It would be much easier to think the guy is a criminal, you know?"

Agatha looked away, notably bored.

"Fine. Pull it together, Trace. Got the message loud and clear." Trace reached over and petted Agatha's white, furry head. "You always know the right thing to say, my friend."

By the time she reached the hotel, Trace had adjusted her attitude. It helped to hear Harry Connick Jr. belting out "It's Beginning to Look a Lot Like Christmas" as she slid her purse and lunch bag under the desk, feeling ready for a new day.

"You got a message from The Palms," Hannah said, handing her a slip of paper.

Trace plucked the pink memo from the front desk clerk's hand. "Thanks. Heard they're going through some renovations, and it's a good thing too. What's our occupancy? They're going to want to know."

"We're at seventy-five percent. Not bad."

"Wow. Good for us."

Hannah shrugged. "It's Christmas and the sun's out. Sounds like a party to me."

"Right? That's what I always say. Forget snow. The beach is better for the holidays."

"Agreed." Hannah lingered, frowning. "Question. Don't you think that checking a competing property for their occupancy rate seems, I don't know, counterintuitive?"

"Ah, but that's what I love about it," Trace said, referring to the weekly practice with all the hotels in the area. "It's a nod to a bygone era. We help each other, iron sharpening iron and all that."

"Somebody's chipper today."

"What can I say? The holidays can do that to a person."

Priscilla Prince sashayed into the hotel and approached the desk. She lowered her sunglasses. "Good afternoon, Trace."

"Hi, Priscilla. You're a bombshell today. Working?"

Priscilla laughed in that free-as-a-bird way of hers. "Darling, Trace. You are such a soothing balm to my middle-aged soul."

Those who didn't know Priscilla might think all that

joy was because she married a billionaire, but it's not true. When she first came to the inn, she was in the midst of a big heartache. Then she began working as a hairdresser in the spa, and everyone loved her. Even after all that, she *still* comes to work every so often, like today.

"Don't talk to me about middle age!" Trace said. "I have a milestone birthday coming up and—"

Priscilla abruptly blew Trace a kiss and said, "Ta-ta, darling." She walked in the direction of the spa so quickly that if she didn't slow down, she might just be in danger of tripping on her backless pumps.

"Trace?"

She whipped a look around to find the big boss's wife, Meg, in front of her. Meg began working for the inn years ago. Now she was the sales and marketing vice president *and* married to one of the owners. "Hi, there."

"I could use your help. My group of twelve wants to move out of the conference room and into the restaurant for the meal portion of their meeting. Would you—"

"Double check that the restaurant has their stuff together?"

Meg grinned and tapped her clipboard on the counter. "Knew I could count on you."

"Of course, you can." When Meg turned to leave, Trace said, "Looked like a fun gathering last night."

"Gathering?"

"I saw Liddy's post on Insta. Dinner out with the girls?"

"Oh, right. Yes. Just a quick bite. You know how it is."

No, actually, I don't ...

Thomas blew by then, shooting her with fake finger pistols and meowing. Meg raised her brows.

Trace smirked. She ignored him, instead casting another look at Meg. "So anyway, did you have a nice time?"

"Hey, Trace," Thomas interrupted. "You and your cat have big plans for the weekend?" He laughed like a silly child instead of a thirty-something adult.

"Nothing that includes you," she grumbled.

Meg looked from Trace to Thomas and laughed lightly. "Oh, Thomas." She glanced at the phone on the concierge desk where a red light blinked. "I'll let you get to that." Before she left, she tapped the desk with her hand. "Thanks for your help with the group tonight."

Trace picked up the receiver. "Concierge desk, Trace speaking."

"Just the woman I'd like to speak to."

"And who might you be?"

The man chortled. "Samuel Chambers here. Or to you, Sam."

Trace paused. Chambers owned The Palms, a rather rinky-dink property compared to Sea Glass Inn, if you asked her. Though she had always thought the place had good bones. That was something.

"They've got the big man on campus calling for room occupancy these days?"

His laugh reverberated in her ears. "That's what I've always admired about you, Trace Murphy. You're a woman who says what she means. You didn't pull any punches there."

More like, says whatever's on the top of her head—not always the same thing.

Samuel Chambers had been around for years. If the stories were to be believed, he and the original Mr. Riley—Jackson's father—were best friends until a golf bet or something soured them on each other.

Sad.

"Front desk tells me we're at seventy-five percent today. How is today shaping up for your site?"

"I'll pass that along to my staff. That's not why I'm calling, Ms. Murphy."

Hm. If he wasn't calling for the weekly numbers, what in the world did he want?

"I'd like to invite you to lunch." His voice boomed. "What do you say to that?"

Trace blinked. That old coot Samuel asking her on a date? He had to be, what, forty years older than her? She might not have had a date in a while—since Priscilla's wedding, to be exact—but she wasn't desperate enough to go out with a man who might need her to cut his food for him!

Or maybe ... maybe he was just being nice? Rats. She cleared her throat. "Thank you for the lovely offer, Samuel, but I am on the afternoon shift today, so no lunch break for me."

"Pity."

"It was a nice ... thought." She gave her head a small shake, but unfortunately, caught eyes with Thomas as she did. He gave her large googly eyes back.

"Ah, but I do not give up easily," Samuel said, snagging her attention again. "Name the date. I have something I would like to speak to you about that I believe you will be interested in. Go ahead. I'll wait."

She frowned, leafing through her calendar. So she was old school? Paper worked for her. "I'm not interested in a reverse mortgage or anything, if that's what you're selling. And I say that respectfully."

Sam's garbled laughter rattled the phone line. "Your repartee never fails to disappoint!"

Repartee?

"Okay, Trace, let's cut to the chase, shall we? I would like to offer you a job."

She stilled. "You want to offer me ..."

"That's right. We'll need to talk about the particulars, of course. But I'm sure you'll be pleased. It's too good of an offer for you to turn down. I'll tell you about it at lunch. What do you say?"

Trace was too taken aback to say much of anything—a rarity for her. She swallowed, trying to think, when she sensed the arrival of a guest at her desk. She lifted her chin to find Noah watching her. His eyes crinkled at the corners, and he wore a quiet, patient smile that gave her the impression he had all the time in the world.

Despite the sudden and inconvenient thudding of her heart, she held up a finger as if to say *Just a sec,* and returned her attention to the call. "Okay, Samuel, yes, lunch would be fine. Say, tomorrow?"

"Meet me at Ventanas. Noon sharp." *Click.*

Slowly, she put down the phone.

"Hi, Trace. Intense guest?"

Trace nodded slowly. A shift had occurred, a slow dawning that the invisibility cloak she had unwittingly been wearing for much of her life was slowly fading. Someone had noticed her enough to track her down and offer her a job, and more importantly, Noah, the stud, remembered her name.

Yes, things were most definitely looking up.

"Something ... something like that." She smiled and didn't have to force it this time.

He leaned across the counter and set a box in front of her. "I think I ruined your quiet time last night. So I brought you a peace offering."

Catch me now, Cowboy. I'm swooning ...

"Go on and open it."

A gift? Trace tilted her head, examining it. She slid her gaze back up to Noah.

"It's not a booby trap."

"I'm not sure if people use the word *booby* anymore."

His face turned a light shade of red. Poor guy. Trace wasn't exactly the type to hold back, even if that wasn't what she wanted to say. What she *wanted* to say was ... will you marry me?

Then again, she didn't really know this man, only spoke to him that one time in the chapel. And if she were honest, she thought he might be a criminal of sorts, though she'd never actually said so out loud.

That was a plus, right?

Would accepting this gift from him be a little like taking candy from a stranger?

Noah shook his head and reached for the box, as if to give up.

"Hold on there, *pardner*." Trace, too, reached out,

bumping her fingers into his as she pulled it away from him.

He chuckled. "I was just going to offer to open it for you, not steal it away." Noah winced. "Maybe not the best choice of words."

"Because I accused you of stealing last night?" She did it again ... said too much.

"Are you going to open it or not?"

Trace nodded, pulled the top off the box, and released a sigh. "My goodness!"

"You like it?"

Her face warmed. "A Christmas tree made of sea glass." She pulled her gaze from the artsy trinket. "It's beautiful."

"I thought so."

"I hope you didn't pay retail for it."

He chuckled. "What if I did?"

She thought about that. So extravagant. She was a regular at several secondhand shops downtown and quite proud of that. So when was the last time she'd gotten something special that wasn't from a thrift store?

Her fingertips brushed across the colorful branches made of glass tumbled by waves—translucent green and blue with a white and red topper. "Red glass is pretty rare."

"Is it?"

She nodded, caught between wanting to thank him profusely and tell him the gift was the prettiest thing she'd ever seen. Or, if she were being downright truthful with herself, the big question in her mind was, *What's the catch?*

Chapter 3

Simply Having a Wonderful Christmastime

For her lunch appointment with Samuel Chambers, Trace wore dark glasses and a scarf à la Audrey Hepburn. After all, they were dining on the heated patio of the most exclusive—aka expensive—restaurant in the beachside city, so she wanted to at least try and look the part. She had found both accessories at her favorite thrift store close to the mission downtown.

Another good reason for a quasi-disguise: she didn't want to be noticed by anyone from Sea Glass Inn. Her position at the inn was at-will, but she still felt a little sheepish for agreeing to meet a man about a job.

Sam smiled kindly at her. "Are you ready to join our team, Trace?"

"Sam, I am flattered to be asked. VP of Operations is—"

"It's right up your alley, is what it is. Say yes."

He was being sincere. The near-octogenarian had been both gregarious and serious during their meal, regaling her with stories of his only child, as well as his beloved, deceased wife. "You remind me of my daughter, Kelly, when she was your age. She has a mind of her own and speaks it, much like you."

Trace took his musings as a compliment, though she'd come to figure out over time that others didn't always take her responses as well. He told her how he wanted to build up his own resort in this small seaside town. "My wife would have loved to see it," he said.

Trace removed her sunglasses, allowing the cozy brightness of winter sunlight in. "You drive a hard bargain, Sam. So ... I'm going to say maybe."

He nodded. "Thought you might." He turned up his palms but nodded anyway. "Still loyal to old Riley."

The inn's original owner passed away several years ago, but his kindness and patience had left a lasting impression on Trace. "Thank you for understanding."

On the way out of the restaurant, Sam turned to her. "They don't appreciate you over at Sea Glass the way I will. Think about the benefits. Promise me that?"

Later, after Trace had made that promise, she wandered into the inn. Today was her day off. She wanted the mystery paperback that she'd bought after being caught with Steph's swashbuckler novel—couldn't let that happen again. She'd planned to read it during lulls at the desk, but those turned out to be non-existent.

"Didn't expect to see you here," Noah said, as he strode up next to her. "Almost didn't recognize you behind those glasses. Hepburn?"

The effect of Noah's voice on her insides was ... unexpected. A chill ran through her. In a good way. She refused to allow the quake of her insides to show, though. Instead, she lowered her oversized sunglasses, gave him a look, and said, "Hey."

Noah grinned. His gaze met hers.

Man. He was spectacular. Piercing eyes, casual stubble, an earnest smile. And he recognized Audrey in her disguise, another plus. She worked to keep her expression as unimpressed as possible. It wasn't easy.

"Doing some modeling today?" he asked.

Trace laughed. "You didn't tell me you were a salesman."

"What made you say that?"

"That slick compliment you were slinging my way."

"I was being sincere." He held a fist to his chest. "I'm hurt."

"L.O.L."

"So," he said, his eyes brushing down her face, "what are you doing here on your day off, looking like Audrey Hepburn?"

"I—"

Thomas butted in between them. She wanted to smack the valet, who apparently had no idea that the man she was talking to was a guest. And that he was currently looking right into her soul.

"Can I help you, Thomas?"

"Yeah, I was just wondering if you'd heard the news."

"News?"

"The circus is in town and they're fresh out of bearded ladies. Hurry—you still have time." He cackled like a fool.

Usually, this was when Trace would toss Thomas a

withering stare and throw in a quip of her own. Something about not tripping on his shoelaces on the way out.

She didn't exactly enjoy the banter he so regularly foisted upon her, but she had tolerated it. For years, really. As an only child, she figured Thomas's treatment was akin to an older brother who couldn't stop teasing his younger siblings. Only Thomas was younger than her.

Still, she never let it bother her. But right now, it did. She wasn't a crier, but a hot sense of tears pressed against the back of her eyes, and pressure scurried down her sinuses. Try as she might, she couldn't think of one smart-mouthed thing to say back to Thomas. Still, she opened her mouth. She had to try …

But before the tears came, before words of rebuke formed in her head, a warm hand enveloped hers. Thomas disappeared from view and Noah's arms, strong as she imagined they might be, pulled her against him. He stared into her eyes, then let his gaze lower ever so briefly to her mouth.

Butterflies flitted around her head. A hundred drunken butterflies, their wings furiously fanning the heat from her skin. If this was her reaction to a near-kiss, she couldn't imagine what she would do if she ever experienced a real one.

The huskiness of his voice rumbled in his chest—she felt every volcanic movement. "Scram," he was saying to invisible-to-her Thomas. "She's beautiful—leave her alone."

"Yes, sir."

Trace swayed. Noah must have sensed her inability to stand. Gently, he inched them both to the concierge desk.

Noah released her from his embrace, and mercifully, waited a beat before completely letting go. Trace reached for the counter and leaned against it, as if there had been no sudden disruption in her day.

Noah glanced over his shoulder, then swung his gaze back to her. He tilted his head down, his brow furrowed, a whisper on his lips. "Don't let that guy get to you anymore, okay?"

"Mm-hm."

He flashed her a grin. "Pretty sure we just took care of that, though. You aren't upset with me, I hope."

"Upset?"

"For swooping in to save you. Not that you *needed* saving. You strike me as someone who could put that guy in his place with a few word darts of your own." He gestured toward the valet with his thumb. He was now yards away. "But Trace, he shouldn't be speaking to you that way."

"Uh, yeah, well, I mean, he and I ..." She sighed, her vision coming into focus. Noah's attention had been an act of mercy. Well, *of course,* it had been an act. He'd already shown her his generosity by bringing her a gift yesterday. Best tip she'd ever received, and there had been many over the years. Innocuous little gifts left by patrons who had appreciated her service. Nothing more.

Her scarf had slipped, so she slid it back onto her head and secured it beneath her chin. The aura of elegance had faded, and though she lifted her chin in defiance at its disappearance, Trace half-expected to be handed a bucket and mop.

That's when she spotted Meg and Liddy across the

lobby, gawking at her and Noah. She considered both women friends, though they held titles that clearly held rank over hers. But friends, just the same.

Only ... they had both been acting strange lately. Maybe it was her imagination. Or maybe she really had become invisible to them and others at the inn. (Except Thomas. How she wished she could become invisible to him ...)

She snapped another look up at Noah. His crystal blue eyes connected with hers, and he raised one brow.

"I have a proposition for you." She gave him a small smile. "Wanna hear it?"

❉

"You want me to pretend that I'm your boyfriend." He examined her face, looking for any sign of a *gotcha* coming.

"Just while you're a guest here. Only a few weeks, right?"

"Right." His mind turned the prospect over.

"It's just ..." The fire he'd seen in her eyes waned. She was struggling but continued. "It's hard to explain."

He could do this, of course, pretend for a while. But after that almost-kiss, he would no doubt be facing tempta-tion regularly. He'd have to work hard to snuff that out. "May I ask why? Is it because of that—?"

"Valet?" She clucked her tongue and waved a hand in the air. "He's harmless."

His mind drifted to his impulsive move in the lobby. Man, he wanted to punch that guy who kept teasing Trace but figured violence would have been frowned upon at the upscale resort.

So instead, he reached for Trace, thought briefly about kissing her—yeah, he did—but at the last second caught himself. The hug he pulled her into might have been brief, but he'd felt sucker punched ever since. He was man enough to admit that ... to himself, anyway.

Despite the innocent nature of it all, he'd seen fireworks. Had both seen and heard them high in the sky of his mind. His parents once spent Bastille Day in France, and his mother often liked to describe the starry-eyed revelers calling out in the night, *Ooh, la, la!* over and over again.

Funny how that story came to him at this moment. Ooh, la, la was right. Double ooh, la, la that she hadn't decked him for swooping in to rescue her from that big, bad valet. As usual, he hadn't thought his actions through. Well, until the last second. Noah had been scolded for that his entire life. It would not have surprised him if Trace had clocked him. He deserved it.

But she didn't. Au contraire, to coin another French phrase—she surprised him by clinging to him. At least, that's how he interpreted her lack of shrinking back in horror.

Only ... she had been playacting too. Her proposition now to keep up the charade proved that. And with that sudden understanding, the fireworks sputtered. *Oomph la la...*

Noah refocused on Trace, whose expression had changed. It now registered defeat. "I see," she was saying. "You don't want to."

It wasn't that he didn't want to pretend they were a

couple. He was more worried about keeping himself in check. They had only known each other a few days, but already he could see that Trace was a woman who knew what she wanted. And right now, she wanted to be ... seen.

And what did he want?

Easy. He wanted to help her.

"Not true," he said. Another completely different thought plowed into his mind: How had he never, ever thought of this ploy before? What a perfect way this might have been to get his parents to, finally, *back off.*

Noah meant that most respectfully, of course.

He chuckled. If he had been on the ball, he might have even taken his fake girlfriend to Maine, snow and all. Without the constant matchmaking, maybe an ice-cold winter wouldn't have been so bad. Then again, how might his ex have handled that ...?

"You're laughing at me," she said.

"I am not."

"You chuckled."

He smiled. "Chuckling is for old men. I was showing appreciation for the thought that ran through my head."

"Which was?"

Did he dare share his mother's penchant for match-making with her? So far they'd enjoyed a kind of detached friendship that might just be what he needed in his life right now. Well, except for the near lip-lock from earlier. But that had served its purpose for them both. And they had each moved on (hopefully).

"I was thinking about how your offer takes concierge service to a higher level." So he wasn't quite ready to divulge too much of his personal life?

"I aim to please—you've got that right."

They both laughed at that. He pounded a light fist onto the concierge desk. "I'll do it on one condition."

"Which is?"

"You have dinner with me tonight."

She tilted her head. "Okay. Sure. As long as we go halfsies."

"I invited you. You can't insist on paying."

"I'm insisting on paying *half*."

He knew she was right. This wasn't a date, it was an *arrangement*. His head told him that was a good thing, but his heart was arguing with him. Silently, he told his heart to shove it. If dating apps had taught him anything, it was that he was an old soul—one that needed to learn new ways. What his parents had no longer existed. People didn't meet at work or in church, fall in love, and live happily ever after. Nowadays you had to narrow down your attraction via an app. Then try out a whole lot of people until, maybe, you find someone you can stand to live with.

Romance by chance, that's how he saw it.

He brushed his gaze across her determined face. In some ways, he was thankful for this distraction with Trace. This could work. They'd both have fun but with a firm end date on the horizon. One where no one would get hurt. The whole thing would be over the minute he checked out of the Sea Glass Inn. He'd help her, and honestly, she would be helping him too. Noah needed to prove that he could stay detached in a relationship.

The last woman he had dated could have saved him a lot of heartache if she'd told him upfront she wasn't looking for forever. At least now he knew exactly what he was getting into: a fake relationship and nothing more.

Trace peered out the window. Noah had insisted on picking her up at her apartment in his truck. She'd never had a guest do that before, then again, this was a date, right? At least it was supposed to look like one and that's what guys did—picked up their dates. From what she'd read, anyway, as she hadn't had much experience with all that.

Trace sat across the table from Noah at the hillside restaurant finishing dinner and hoping he wasn't a criminal. Even more so, an axe murderer, especially now that he knew where she lived.

He was watching her with a question in his eyes.

"Sorry?" She dabbed her mouth with a napkin.

"I was just saying that it sounds like this isn't the first time the Sea Glass Inn has been shrouded in mystery."

She shook her head a little, remembering what they'd just been talking about before her mind went elsewhere. "No, it is not. Sadly, I wasn't paying attention last time. Liddy was the one sleuthing around, suspecting something was up."

"Liddy. She's ...?"

"Public relations manager. She started at the inn a few years ago. Had some serious health problems but overcame all that. Always said it was like walking on sea glass. It's a story in itself."

Amusement lit his face. She should stop talking but her nerves were in charge of her lips.

"Anyway, Liddy's hunches weren't exactly correct, but something definitely was up with the restaurant, and she almost lost her best friend over the whole mess."

He tilted his head and ruffled his brow, once again reminding her of Ryan Gosling with a big question mark over his head. She hid a smile. "I'm talking about Meg."

"Meg's ... the owner's wife?"

"Hooey, yes. That's a story too. You wouldn't believe it if I sprang it on you. Suffice it to say, Meg nearly got run out of here when Jackson came back to the inn after his father died. She ended up in Italy, of all places. Thankfully, he recovered some sense and ran after her."

Noah chuckled.

"Again with the chuckling. Are you bored?"

He leaned forward, making the space between them more intimate. "On the contrary, Trace. I find you fascinating."

She narrowed her eyes at him, searching for sarcasm. Instead, he was watching her intently. Some people's gazes seemed to flit about when she was talking, but Noah's eyes didn't waver from hers and she was beginning to feel, well, *unclothed*. She bit her lip to keep herself from revealing too much about herself, knowing that vulnerability could not be recovered. Besides, she reasoned, a guy that looked like Noah had likely used that same look on other women.

"So," she said, "tell me about your family."

Both of Noah's eyebrows lifted. "My ... family."

"Yes. Brothers? Sisters? Where are they and why aren't they demanding you come home for Christmas?"

Noah took a bite of steak and chewed it slowly. More than once she'd noticed the intensity in his watchfulness and she couldn't look away. Finally, he put his fork down. "I'm an only child."

She perked. "Really? Me too." That last phrase popped out before she could stop it. What had she just promised herself about saying too much?

"My parents have decided to spend Christmas in the snow again this year, so I opted to stay where the sun's out."

"Can't say that I blame you. I mean, snow is pretty to look at and all, but brrr, so cold."

"Exactly." He took a sip of water and put his glass back down on the table. "I'll be out of here soon enough, and if my mother has something to say about it, we'll be celebrating Christmas together after the new year."

She nodded, not wanting to think that far ahead.

When she didn't offer more conversation, Noah leaned forward again. "Tell me something. You didn't really think I was going to steal from the inn, now did you?"

Trace smirked, biting the inside of her cheek. He probably thought she was being paranoid too. "I don't know what to think, really."

"Seriously?"

She shrugged.

"Do you often go out to dinner with thieves?"

"Not that I know of, but what can I say? I know where you're staying."

He chuckled. "True."

After they'd eaten, the waiter cleared their plates and

offered dessert. They decided on key lime pie and two forks.

He took a bite of pie. "You really love the inn, don't you."

She shrugged. "It's a job, one I've held for more than a decade."

He pressed on. "And that's why you're so devoted to it?"

Trace thought about that. Of all the people from the inn that they'd talked about tonight—and the many they hadn't—how many cared whether they found her face at the concierge desk—or someone else's?

A boldness came over her. "I'm not so sure devoted is the right word. I'm committed, and I take that very seriously."

"I see that. You're loyal." He speared another bite of pie.

"But that doesn't mean commitment doesn't have an expiration date."

Noah looked up sharply.

She continued. "That's why I'm thinking of taking another job."

"Really? Where?"

"Not important." She wasn't ready quite yet to divulge many details. "But I've been offered a good position elsewhere, and, well, I'm thinking about it."

He nodded but was quiet. Eventually, "You know your worth. That's admirable because many don't value themselves. They continue on, doing the same things year after year, never stopping to consider if making a break could be the best decision they ever made."

"So you've been there."

He seemed to consider that, but only offered her a non-committal shrug. "It's more of an observation."

The quiet tone of his voice made her want to reach out and brush her fingers over his face. She might not have much experience with this dating thing, but these urges seemed to be coming on their own volition. Maybe experience was overrated.

Trace put her hands in her lap. Her proposition to ask a near-stranger to pretend to be her boyfriend suddenly felt silly, like something straight out of a holiday rom-com. At the time, when Thomas had embarrassed her for the umpteenth time and Noah had swooped in to fix that, it seemed like a good idea.

But now she was having to hold her own hands in her lap to keep them from doing something they shouldn't. Her mouth went dry, but she didn't dare extricate her fingers. Thankfully, a server stopped to clear their dessert dish away, giving them one more reprieve from connecting.

Don't fall in love, Trace. Do. Not. Fall. In. Love. She repeated the mantra in her head. Falling in love would be a tragic outcome of their agreement. Trace forced herself to think about that. Though she was very much living in the here and now, Noah was already bringing up the new year, when he'd be far away from here.

No, falling in love would never do.

Noah placed his napkin to the side of his plate. "Let's walk off dinner on the beach."

"Tonight? Now?"

"I live inland, remember? You wouldn't want to deprive me of an evening walk on the sand, would you?"

She hesitated, but only for a second. "Far be it from me."

Outside, though wrapped in jackets, they both slipped out of their shoes and let them dangle from their fingers. Their bare feet sank into the cool sand. Trace tripped on driftwood sticking out of the sand but caught herself. Warm chills rippled down her spine as Noah casually placed his hand on her back, keeping her steady. So much for trying to keep a safe distance from him.

"Do you have family nearby?" he asked.

"Oddly enough, both of my parents moved to Florida several years ago leaving me to grow up in a hurry."

He chuckled. "How is it odd that they both went?"

"Divorced."

"Ah. May I ask why you didn't join them?"

"I don't like bugs. Or the kind of humidity that makes a person want to shower several times a day."

"I'm not a fan of that either."

"Plus, it's a big state and they're on opposite ends. My dad remarried. She's nice enough, but we never really clicked."

They walked in silence for a while, and when she stumbled for the second time, Noah was there. She'd been proud of the fact that she had managed to (sort of) brush off the intimate moment at the inn the other night. Part of her had wanted to compliment him on his acting skills—Noah had convinced her that he'd wanted to seal his kindness with a kiss, even for just a moment—but then she would find herself thinking too much of how it might feel to be kissed by, well, *him*.

"This is what I'm talking about."

Trace snapped a look at Noah's face. He grinned, looking out toward the horizon. She followed his gaze. The sun had long set, but the glow of stars and moon managed to paint a swath of velvety color and soft light across the darkened sky.

"I don't come out here enough," she said.

"Really? Why not?"

She glanced up at him again. "Beats me. Sometimes I sit outside on my breaks to watch the water awhile, but those are short and my mind's often thinking about ... work."

"Ouch."

"Mm-hm. Didn't realize that until right now." She inhaled a deep breath of salt-scrubbed air. "Guess I've been taking all this sky and sea for granted."

"It's easy to do, get sucked into work, I mean. But let me tell you, Trace, while I'm here, I'm going to make it a point to admire the coast every chance I get." He lowered his gaze to hers. "It'll be over before I know it."

Something twisted in Trace's chest, mimicking a shot of pain. There he went again, talking about leaving. All she could add was, "Yeah," before turning her gaze once again back toward the sea. Three weeks was suddenly a very, *very* short time.

Chapter 4

My Only Wish (This Year)

Too bad she wasn't going to let herself fall in love with Noah Bridges. He was her type, though she didn't realize until now that she even had one. Trace bit the inside of her mouth while scrutinizing the lobby tree where a gaping hole had formed.

"There's nothing wrong with that tree." Hans frowned. He'd been standing beside her, pestering her about guest details she had already handled.

Trace stuck a star-shaped ornament into the empty spot and sighed. "It's got holes, Hans. Can't have that." Her mind continued to be bombarded with thoughts of Noah. He checked all the boxes waiting to be filled, all right. Well, except for the fact that he didn't live here and his hug at the concierge desk was an act of charity (i.e. fake).

But otherwise, he would have been perfect for her.

Last night, they walked on the beach for an hour, and in that time, she learned that he preferred not to talk about work at night, enjoyed a good board game—they'd already made plans to beat each other at Scrabble—and sometime in the last year, he'd been dumped. Though when she had nudged him to expand on that, he changed the subject.

Her heart broke a little when the admission tumbled out of his mouth as they were walking down the long stretch of beach, listening to waves rolling onto shore in the dark. Her reaction to his pain took her by surprise too.

Trace might not have dwelled too much on that right now if Hans hadn't walked up to her minutes ago, full of questions. She added another ornament, this one a hula snowman, to a branch as he rounded the corner. He examined the tree, as if still judging it.

"For goodness sake, Hans, here." She scooped up a handful of tinsel and handed some to him. "Go on. Add a little pizzazz."

He looked at the clump of shimmery decorations in his hand like it was limp broccoli. "What am I supposed to do with this?"

"Put it on the tree." She demonstrated by tossing a few strands of tinsel onto bare branches. "It's not brain surgery."

He dumped the tinsel back into its box, then dusted off his hands. "Not for me. My wife and kids handle this at home."

"Makes sense."

He leveled a stony gaze at her.

"All I meant is that somebody has to be the grinch of the family and—tag—you're it."

"What happened to that guy you were hanging around with at Priscilla's wedding?"

She frowned and tossed more tinsel onto the tree. "Kind of an out-of-the-blue question there, Hans." She kept her eyes on the tree, examining it for more holes where decorations should be. "Why the sudden interest in my love life?"

The front desk manager shrugged. "Not really sudden." Hans wore a suit no matter the time of year, and she sometimes wondered if the collar was too tight because he always did this funny little lift of his chin and neck swivel, as if he was trying to escape it. Like right now.

"Well, if you must know, that just didn't work out."

"Shame. You two seemed like a good match."

She puckered her face. Trace had met Rowan when he delivered flowers to Priscilla in the spa one day. She'd had to walk him over there since he seemed to be having trouble understanding her directions and kept showing up back at the concierge desk for her to repeat them.

Who knew that was his flirty way to keep seeing her?

One thing led to another and they went out a few times. Trace even invited him to attend Priscilla's wedding with her, and he showed up looking quite steampunk in a frock coat and horn-rimmed glasses. A week later, he announced she was "too quirky" for him and said they should move on.

"I mean that sincerely, Trace." Hans paused, and she sensed more was coming. "You know, it would behoove you to be careful not to overstep your bounds where hotel guests are concerned."

Trace narrowed her eyes, and not just because he had used the word *behoove* in a sentence in the twenty-first century. She'd have to remember that one for her future Scrabble date with Noah.

He continued. "I suspect there's a policy about, you know, dating hotel guests."

She laughed outright at this. "There's a *policy* about who I decide to date?"

"Well, I don't know if it's in writing or anything." He did that funny little move with his shirt collar again. "But it should be."

"Uh-huh."

"You don't agree?"

"Well, I don't know, Hans. I can understand corporations that frown on employees dating each other, and government entities, say the FBI, having a no-contact policy between staffers." She moved a sparkly ornament to a higher branch, where it belonged. "But to say that I cannot spend time with a person who happens to be a hotel guest? Pretty sure the romance channel would have to disagree with you on that one."

"Romance channel!"

"Only the most-watched network during the holidays. A policy like you're suggesting would kill an awful lot of meet-cutes, and we just can't have that now, can we?" She patted his shoulder, though she would have rather smacked his pinched face. Just a little. "I'm sure you understand."

Hans's face flushed. Admittedly, the conversation had turned too personal, but he started it. What was it to Hans whom she dated? She should be infuriated at the front desk manager's nosiness. But the thought of having someone like Noah in her life buoyed her enough to overlook Hans's questions.

He grabbed a tissue from the concierge counter and sopped his brow. Hannah approached. "I need a break. Cover the desk, Hans?"

Trace liked that about Hannah—said what she needed and didn't apologize for it. In typical Hans fashion, though, he let out a sigh laced with drama, as if she had just asked him to fetch her coffee and a sweet roll from the cafe. She stood her ground and left for who knew where. Unlike Trace, Hannah liked to take food from the galley downstairs and retreat away from the inn. She was one of the hardest working around here and she probably had her mid-day siestas to thank for that.

If only Trace could shut off so easily. As Hans slunk back to the front desk she replayed his nosiness—and the thoughts that consumed her regarding the guest in the Florence suite.

Her momentary elation about *having someone like Noah in her life* sank as she remembered the truth: their relationship would expire soon. Noah had said as much last night, and though she had tried to hide away that little nugget of truth, it continued to poke its way toward the light—like a stubborn weed that would bend, but not break.

A guest approached the concierge desk. The man wore a beret and lime green polyester slacks. He had *tee time* written all over his face.

Trace shook off her musings and flashed him a smile. She returned to her spot behind the desk, all the while determining that she would hold onto the fun with Noah much like the holidays: live them to the fullest.

And when they were over? She would deal with the

fallout then.

"You think guests are stealing from the inn?"

"I didn't say that."

"Then ... they're not stealing."

Trace looked up from the game of Monopoly they had set up in the living room of his suite. Noah tried to deny the jolt that simple brush of her eyes sent through his body. "I'm not sure who's doing the pilfering," she said, "but it's happening. Housekeeping has been tallying up the missing items, but I know they include towels, coffee makers, irons, and weirdly, some table lamps.

He swallowed and forced his mind back to the game—and the issue that seemed to be needling her. "But nobody seems to care."

"Right."

Noah passed go and promptly collected two hundred dollars. "Well, I care."

Trace rolled the dice and landed on a jailbird. She snapped a look at him. "Just visiting."

He chuckled. "Of course."

"I've got my eye on a beautiful place just up around the corner."

"And ... she shows her hand."

"You wouldn't!"

Noah grinned but didn't answer her. They were supposed to be playing Scrabble, but she'd brought both games with her and what was he supposed to say? He was a sucker for real estate, both real and imagined.

"Ooh, ooh! Turn that up." Trace pointed toward the speaker on the credenza. He'd set it to Christmas music and, until now, it had served as background to their banter.

He pulled out his phone, found the music app, and turned up the volume on "Have Yourself a Merry Little Christmas."

"I thought this song was sad," he said.

"Not this version. Francesca Battistelli sings this one and it's much better, in my opinion."

He listened to a couple of lines, pursing his lips and nodding as he did.

"See what I mean?" she said. "The old line was 'if the fates allow.'"

"Ah, but instead she said, 'if the Lord allows.'" He bobbed his head. "Huh. I like that."

"Me too. I read a long time ago that the writer became a Christian and changed the lyrics. Not too many sing this version, though."

"I'm not sure I've ever heard it, but maybe I wasn't paying attention. Always thought 'fates' was a weird idea."

"Right? I mean, fate is like, I don't know, make-believe or something."

He stared at her for a beat. "We have more in common than I thought, Trace."

She reached for the dice, but he playfully pushed her hand away.

She gasped, then let loose a quick laugh.

Watching her with a dare on his face, Noah tossed the dice and made it swiftly down a row. He loved this part and hated to admit that his heart revved a little as he moved more quickly toward his goal.

Trace took her turn next, picking up B&O Railroad. Though it was a real place, he always thought that the guy who named that square had a sense of humor. He moved forward.

She cleared her throat. "Getting back to what we were talking about ... is that why you said you cared?"

"Cared about ...?"

"Care whether or not someone is stealing from the inn?"

He frowned while she took another turn. "Clearly you are still questioning my morals like you did that night in the chapel."

She laughed. "So sensitive. I was just curious who was in the chapel after dark."

"Ha! Right. You took one look at me and thought I was a hoodlum."

Trace's mouth parted and hovered there, like she had something to say to that but was holding back. It took some doing for him to keep his gaze off her rose-tinged lips.

Finally, she smiled. "Who says I thought twice about you?"

If he had not been looking at her, had only heard those words said aloud, he might have thought she was being churlish. But he saw the playfulness in her gaze, like dancing light in her eyes, and knew—she'd been thinking of him all right.

But did he want to follow the path to where those thoughts took them? Regrettably, no. Investing his heart again only to see it ripped to shreds was not something he wanted to sign up for again. *Do not pass go this time, buddy.*

Trace had made it clear when they'd made their pact that this was a temporary situation. She hadn't said this, but it was becoming increasingly obvious to him that Trace felt somewhat invisible around here. Or, in the case of that doofus valet—bullied. He couldn't for the life of him figure out why that would be the case. She was funny, honest, hard-working.

And beautiful. His heart twisted slightly as the word made its way through his mind.

"I've hurt your feelings."

He looked up to see that the words on Trace's lips were a question that she wasn't sure she knew the answer to. A flit of disbelief crossed her expression, as if she questioned whether she had the power to do what she said—hurt his feelings.

She hadn't, of course. He was perceptive enough to know that, contrary to what she said, she *had* been thinking about him that night in the chapel, wondering who he was and why he was there. Maybe she was even wondering something more ...

But clearly, she had not hurt his feelings.

He raised his brows at her. "Not at all. I was thinking about your earlier question. You asked why I cared about what happened to the inn."

"Yes, I did."

He shrugged. "I care because ... stealing is wrong." His heart rate increased, and Noah was finding it difficult to erase the smile burgeoning on his face. He reached across the board and plunked down play money to buy Park Place. "And clearly, that agitates you."

She gasped. "You knew I was saving up for that!"

He quirked a smile. "That's what I love about you. A fighter for justice *and* competitive too."

Maybe he shouldn't have used the word *love*. Abruptly, Trace stood and started pacing back and forth on the deck.

Still, he tried to make light of it. "Something I said?"

"What if the criminals are guests with a big agenda?"

"Um—"

She turned and stopped, reminding him of a sleuth his mother would watch on television. "You know, people who check in on a coupon then dash into open rooms while the maids are cleaning and take what they see."

"Well—"

"Or maybe a gang of them. I mean, we've got some good deals during the holidays. Maybe they check in, pilfer, then sell the goods on the internet."

"It's all possible."

"Could you ...?"

"Keep my eyes open?"

Trace sat back down and looked deeply into his eyes. He hovered in that place between cool casual and pulling her into a passionate embrace, far different from that little show he gave in the lobby.

"Would you?" she asked, her expression hopeful.

Would I take you in my arms right now and give you a real kiss? Offer you a giant step up from that embarrassing false alarm I gave you in the hotel lobby?

Instead, he shrugged. "Sure. I'll watch out for women walking by with bulging purses and guys carrying TVs on their shoulders."

Trace punched him. "You're a real funny guy, aren't you?"

He rubbed the spot on his shoulder where she'd socked him, faking injury. "And you're a harsh taskmaster."

"You have no idea, my friend. No idea at all."

He laughed at the way she said it, her voice quirky yet earnest. They finished up their game, and when she stood to go, Noah lunged for Scrabble and tempted her with it like a piping hot pizza.

"One game?"

She stuck a fist into her tiny waist. "That's all it'll take for me to pin your tail to the wall, you know."

He laughed. Right. Had he mentioned his father had been a high school English teacher and that he would always make him rewrite his papers a dozen times? Probably not.

Noah watched as Trace padded over to the suite's refrigerator and pulled out a couple of Perriers like she lived there. He glanced at the game, suddenly wanting to kick it to the floor in favor of doing something altogether different.

Oblivious to his momentary insanity, she smiled and handed him fizzy water. She then sat down across from him, a determined look on her face. He grinned back. Challenge accepted.

She began the game with the word t-e-a-s-e-r and Noah realized he was beginning to be drawn to Trace in a way that would be, when the time came, very tough to fight.

"Hey, Hope." Trace dropped some change into the red metal bucket. She'd run out to her car on her break to get some coins because her purse was empty when she dashed into work earlier today. "How are you this morning?"

"Just fine, thank you." The bellringer wore a thick cap and gloves today, and the tip of her nose looked pink.

"Are you cold out here? You kinda look it. Can I get you some coffee?"

Hope hesitated. "No, no. I'm perfectly fine out here."

Trace waved a hand, not accepting her answer. "Cream? Sugar?"

"You really don't have to."

"If you don't tell me, I'll ask the cafe to put almond milk in it or something."

"Cream! Oh, and a wee bit of sugar." The rosiness spread to Hope's cheeks. "If you don't mind."

Trace laughed on her way inside. "I'll order that it be sent out here to you. Give me a minute!"

Coffee ordered and sent out to Hope, Trace returned to the concierge desk. She hadn't seen Noah all day and was already missing him.

This wasn't good at all. Soon enough, he would finish the work he came to do in this town, hop into his truck, and drive off, leaving a cloud of sand in his wake. Less than two weeks away until then. The mantra she took on, the one to not become attached to him, chanted through her head, and yet, here she was, sad she hadn't seen Noah stroll through the lobby at all today.

These unavoidable thoughts followed her around like a dark, gray cloud, but she pressed on for another two hours, doing the work she'd come to do.

"Hey, fish face!"

Trace looked up and immediately gritted her teeth at her mistake. She'd been caught answering Thomas's taunt.

He pointed and laughed.

"Santa Claus is coming to Town" played through the lobby and a small part of her wanted to rip a speaker from its bracket. Thomas sidled up to the counter. "What time is Mr. Arthur's tee time?"

Trace ignored him. The phone rang and she picked it up, her eyes letting Thomas know she wasn't planning to respond. He would have to find out the answer he needed by himself. "Concierge desk. How may I help you?"

"Seriously, Trace," Thomas said, reaching across the counter. "I need to know when the old guy's tee time is."

Trace turned her back. She was too old for this treatment, her looming birthday reminding her of this fact. If only ... if only she could talk to her mother. Agatha was a great listener, but she needed her mother's ear just now. How she wished things were different ...

"Ma'am?" Trace shut her eyes at the sound of the voice coming through the phone. "Sorry. Would you repeat that please?"

"Never mind!" The phone clicked in her ear. She drew in a breath slowly and turned.

Thomas had hopped onto the counter and dragged his belly across the surface. He was rifling through her appointment book. "Such an old schoolmarm you are, still writing stuff down on paper."

"Get off of this desk!" Trace swatted his hand away from the appointment log, which was printed from the computer. He tried to make her sound like an old fool, when really, she was trying to help everyone by printing the daily appointment schedule out for quick reference.

Michael Buble's voice, though warm and wonderful, failed to soothe her as he began belting out "Holly, Jolly Christmas." She'd already heard the song twice today because, no doubt, it was part of a loop that would continue past Christmas Day.

There was neither holly nor jolly in her current mood, though she couldn't exactly say why. She leaned forward and wagged her finger in front of Thomas's face, his expression cocky. "Stop touching my things or I will report you."

Thomas moved her finger from his face, and Trace yanked her hand away. A guest waited nearby, but her cool had turned to a simmer that might have very well rolled into a boil. She opened her mouth to tell Thomas exactly what she thought of him when Liddy appeared at the counter.

"Hello, Mrs. Ortega," Liddy said, her attention on the waiting guest. "What can we do for you?"

Heat filled Trace's cheeks and her gaze darted to the guest and the expectant look on the woman's face. There was little doubt that she had overheard her skirmish with Thomas. What was wrong with her? She never let things get to her like this.

"I would like a dinner reservation for two in the cafe," Mrs. Ortega said.

Trace nodded once, not knowing nor caring what how Thomas would find answers. "I will call the restaurant right now. Would you like patio or dining room seating?"

Liddy walked away, her eyes on Trace, forehead

pinched. She mouthed *Are you okay?* but Trace shook it off and took care of her guest. As always.

As soon as the desk was quiet again, Trace signaled for Hannah to relieve her for a late lunch. She grabbed her purse and stepped away, wandering outside to the grassy knoll outside of the chapel.

The sun had begun its graceful dive toward the sea's horizon. In a few hours, the golden ball would sink into the ocean's blue depths, and those who wandered out to watch it go would breathe a collective sigh. Another day done.

But, for now, there was still work to do and sun to enjoy. She picked up her phone and typed out: *You'd love it here, Mom.* Her fingers hovered over her phone screen, but in the end, she erased her text.

Trace bit the inside of her cheek. She wasn't a fan of pity parties, but with her birthday coming up and the corner she found herself in regarding Noah, she was moving close to throwing herself one complete with streamers, balloons, and a cake so rich she'd have to check her blood sugar after one slice.

If only ... if only things were different where her parents were concerned. Her mother and father split up years ago, and going their separate ways meant she had to pick one. So unfair. She stayed with her mom, which meant she rarely saw her father.

And when she became a teenager? Forget it. She was as interested in him as a liver and onion sandwich.

She hadn't meant to ignore her father all those years, but couldn't he have been the grown-up? She had tried to reconnect with him at one point, but he had gotten married again—to Tammy—and though they both tried, it was almost as if she and her dad had little in common but blood.

Trace sighed and took in the view again, kind of hoping for the night sky to come soon. It reminded her of the other night when she'd walked with Noah under the stars. This was the season for wishes, after all. The good Lord had made sure of that when he sent that beautiful star out in the night to lead those wise men to Him. People had been wishing on stars ever since.

Her wish? There were many ... but it sure would be nice to receive more than a text from her parents on her birthday. Was that too much to ask?

She bit into an apple, its sweetness and crunch like candy on her tongue. In the distance, a V-shaped formation of pelicans searched for their final meal of the day. A twist tugged at her lungs, until she wasn't sure she could take a full breath. So much to think about. It was ... over-whelming.

Sam Chambers had called again, pressing her for an answer about his job offer, and maybe it should be yes. She sucked in more fresh air, letting it fill her lungs and limbs.

Another potential wish came to mind: Noah. She wished they could somehow leap over their pact and be in a real relationship, one with the potential for something more. But he lived and worked far away. And he seemed to be nursing a wound. And ... well, if she thought about it too hard, the list of cons would grow.

Trace never was one to hide her feelings, even from herself. So even though she let her thoughts move to the forefront of her mind, there, locked away in her mind, they would have to stay.

A rumbling in her pocket startled her, as did the name barreling across her screen. She answered the phone tentatively. "Mom?"

"Oh good, I caught you. Yes, Trace, it's me."

The tightness in Trace's neck caught her off guard. Finally. She'd longed to talk to her mom for ages, yet now that the phone call had come, she couldn't think of what to say.

"Trace?"

"Yes? I-I'm on a break from work right now."

"Well, if you don't have time—"

"Wait!" Trace took a breath, calming herself. "I have plenty of time. How are things in Florida?"

"Fantastic. Humidity finally below 60%. I'll take it."

"So you're feeling okay? Work fine?" Trace remembered the last time they had talked, her mom sounded winded. She worried that she worked too much.

"True to both. Since we're both on breaks right now, I'll get to it—I want to make sure you received my text about Christmas."

"I got it."

"Good. Didn't get a call back. Not like you."

"Can I ask you a question?"

"You know you can." As usual, her mother was all business.

"Why don't you ever want to come out for my birthday? Or for Christmas? When you left to move across the country you told me you'd come back every year. But you haven't."

"Trace."

"Mom."

Her mother's weary sigh carried through the receiver. "I've told you this before, my daughter. Criminals don't take a holiday. Not like your guests." She paused. "You know you're always welcome to come here."

"You've never actually said that."

"Do I need to offer my flesh and blood an invitation? Of course, you can come here any time you want. Well, all except this year."

"Cause you're working?"

"Uh, yes, yes. Working."

A giant pause landed between them. Eventually, her mother said, "I meant what I said earlier. Come for a visit or move here, even. And bring that cat of yours!"

"You're allergic."

"I'll get a shot."

"Mom, are you serious?"

Her mother groaned. She'd heard that sound often, though not lately. It meant she was about to end the call.

She beat her mother to it. "Okay, yes, I know that you are serious. Maybe we can talk on Christmas Day. Can we try?"

"Yes, dear. I'd like that."

Trace sat on the bench, replaying her conversation with her mother. So much to unpack. They never seemed to have a typical mother-daughter relationship, but she knew her mother loved her. She had always known that.

Maybe all this unrest was about something altogether different. Trace was about to celebrate another birthday, take another step toward middle age, and until now, hadn't realized how much it scared her. Maybe she had stayed doing the same things day in and day out because it was better than facing change, the kind that comes with growing old.

Is this why she had never asked for a promotion? Or considered moving on to a better position somewhere else (until Sam called)? Or taken a decent vacation?

"Are you okay, Trace?" Noah's warm-as-butter voice said.

She turned, not bothering to brush away the tears that made their way down her cheek. "I'm fine." She blinked. "That's not true. I'm melancholy, but it will pass."

The crease between his eyes deepened. "What happened?"

"Nothing specific. Just the ... same old." When he continued to implore her with sympathetic eyes, she said, "My mother's not coming for Christmas again."

He moved to take the seat beside her but paused. "May I?"

She scooted over, instantly aware of him, the air between them palpable. The intensity of missing him all day deepened.

"Tell me about her."

She shook her head, annoyed that she'd made a big deal of things. "My mother is a crime scene investigator."

"You're kidding."

"I can think of plenty to kid about, but not that. She's busy. Fighting crime is a twenty-four-seven job, you know."

"I don't but I can imagine." He put his arm on the back of the bench and idly played with a strand of her hair. Sent tingles right through her. She should probably swat his hand away, but then again, he was just trying to look the part.

Trace sniffled and wiped her eyes with the crook of her fingers. "I was hoping to see my mother this ... Christmas." She shrugged. "But she can't make it out."

"So you'll be alone this year? Or do you have other family nearby?"

"No family, other than Agatha."

He leaned his head to one side, watching her with inquisitive dark eyes.

"My cat."

"Ah. And your father?"

"Like I mentioned, he married again and they are far away, with a whole mess of pets. He usually texts me on holidays or his wife sends a card. We're not very close."

"I'm sorry."

"It's not a big deal. I have to work almost all of Christmas week anyway."

Noah turned fully toward her now. "I guess seniority doesn't count much in the hospitality industry."

"No, it doesn't. It's a hard week to fill, and they knew they could count on me." She paused and found his eyes with hers. "I'm off on Christmas, though. It's, actually, well, it's my birthday, too."

Both of Noah's brows lifted and a slow smile spread across his face. "You share a birthday with Jesus."

His voice had taken on a reverent tone. Seriously, could he be more perfect? "I do. I never minded and I know he doesn't because it was his idea in the first place!" She cracked a smile, but it quickly dimmed. "It's a big one this year, though. A milestone."

"Really." He appraised her with his gaze but kept his thoughts to himself. Finally, "You gonna tell me, or do I have to butter up someone in HR to break into your employment file?"

Trace inhaled, preparing to let the news out. "I'm going to be thirty-six."

"Thirty ... six?" Noah quirked a grin. "You're a baby! And how is that a milestone?"

"For heaven's sake, it's just one downhill ski run until I'm forty!" Her shoulders drooped and a quiver of a sigh escaped her.

He was still smiling as he said, "Well, I'm closer to forty than you are, and they tell me it's the beginning of a great era in life. I'm choosing to look forward to it."

"Good attitude, Mr. Bridges." She wrinkled her brow. "What about you? You'll still be in the hotel on Christmas. Don't you have family to spend it with?"

Noah removed his arm from the back of the bench. Trace immediately felt a chill of air across her shoulders. She took in the range of emotion flitting across his face. She'd been told once or twice (or three times) that her questions sometimes crossed a line. *Maybe you should dial back the third degree.* Meg had laughed when she'd said those words to her recently, but Trace hadn't taken it too seriously. She probably should have.

"Sorry if that was too nosy."

"It wasn't. I was just playing my answer in my head and not liking the way it sounded."

"Why don't you let me decide how it sounds?"

"Fair enough. My parents, with my mother as instigator, regularly try to fix me up with unsuspecting females."

"Like, on dating apps?"

"Don't give them any ideas!" He laughed outright at

that. "My mother goes about it the old-fashioned way. She's been known to walk right up to women she thinks worthy of becoming her daughter-in-law and show them my photo. How's that for awkward?"

Honestly? She could think of things more awkward than that. Still, his voice registered how horrified his mother's ways made him. She tilted her head, sliding a look at him.

"What would she think of me?"

Noah gave her a small, inquisitive smile. The sinking sunlight illuminated the way his dark eyelashes framed his eyes

"I mean, would she think I was worthy?" She swallowed, watching thoughts form on his face. This line of questioning was, obviously, off limits, but the intimacy of their proximity to each other had bolstered her courage. She could always tell him her question was hypothetical, like their relationship.

"Want to know the truth?"

She lingered before answering. Did she? "I can take it," she said.

He leaned forward, and his gaze brushed down her face. "She would pick you and dump me."

"Oh, you lie."

He chuckled and turned to lean back against the bench and look out to sea. He didn't say it out loud, but the satisfied grin on his face gave her more confidence than she'd had all day. Maybe all year.

Chapter 5

Baby, It's Cold Outside

N oah closed the sliding glass door to his deck, impressed by the firm seal. Overnight, the weather had turned from an obscene display of summer blue to cloud cover over the sea. Oddly, he didn't hate it.

Something else he didn't hate: He had managed to avoid too much personal talk with Trace yesterday.

He had, hadn't he?

Maybe telling Trace about his mother's hobby of trying to find him a wife went too far. In times past, his ability to avoid all things personal would puff him up like an overstuffed turkey. Instead, as his mind replayed their talk and the amount of detail he revealed, he was beginning to deflate. Like one of those floats in New York the day *after* the Macy's Thanksgiving Day parade.

A thought lit up his mind like a summer storm, chasing away the cloud that threatened him. Trace's birthday was coming soon. She'd told him that, but he had made light of it. Hadn't meant to, but he had been having a hard time keeping his composure around her. Pretending should be easy. Piece of cake! Instead, he was coming undone like ice cream set on the dash of his truck.

He checked his phone for texts and emails, grimacing at the spattering of both. And yet, nothing too pressing that he couldn't ignore them for a while and opt for a hot breakfast instead. Obviously, he needed time to collect himself. A full stomach wouldn't hurt either.

After slipping into sweats and a ball cap, Noah wandered down to the cafe on the first floor. He was led to a window overlooking the path that guests could take down to the water. Trace loved that spot. He had noticed that in the short time he'd been staying at the inn.

The cafe was quiet so far this morning, and he didn't mind it. Gave him a chance to think. He ordered hot coffee —something else that would help him with thinking—and a stack of pancakes, and while he ate, Noah watched birds taking flight through the haze.

As he noticed earlier, the day was having trouble deciding what to be. One minute the sun spread a few rays across the sky, and the next, a cloud swallowed it all up.

Trace would not be in today. Although he thought it wise for her to take time off from the busy lobby of this inn, Noah felt irrationally glum at the prospect of not seeing her face. He wasn't the type of guy to think all that much into the future, but hours spent away from his "fake" girlfriend was changing all that. Suddenly, she was on his mind far longer than his problems, and more often than the issues that brought him here, both personal and professional.

It was a problem. Unless ...

He fished his phone out of the pocket of his sweats. He could call her and see if she'd want to do something later. But what? What did a guy propose to do with someone he was pretending to be in a relationship with? It was a dilemma.

His fingers went on autopilot, calling her without his brain knowing what it planned to say.

"Hello?" Her voice sounded groggy.

"Hi there."

"You woke me up to say hi?"

He laughed at the sarcasm in her voice. He was beginning to get used to the sound of it. She yawned audibly. He cleared his throat and spoke low into the phone, suddenly realizing the cafe had begun to fill up.

"Sorry that I woke you," he said.

"Obviously, you can't live without me," she quipped.

He licked his lips. "I've been thinking about your birthday. Since I'll still be here, we should plan something ... special."

"You mean pretend special."

"No, I mean something *really* special. Come on, Trace. It's not every day that a woman turns ... thirty-six."

"Stop teasing me." The rustling in the background sounded like someone turning over in the sheets. Ha—she was still in bed. "So, is this where you ask me where my favorite hot dog stand is?"

"Tell you what. Get out of bed—"

"I'm not in—"

"Lies."

She laughed. "Okay, fine. I might still be resting my eyes a little."

"Well, stop resting and pull on some sweats. I'll meet you on the beach outside the hotel in twenty minutes."

She gasped.

"Don't be late!" He hung up the phone, swigged the rest of his coffee, left the empty mug on the table, then exited into the lobby to the sound of Christmas carols turned up to full volume.

Usually, Trace would avoid the beach on a day like today. Too blustery! Too cold! But considering Noah had given her exactly two-and-a-half minutes to take a shower and head over to meet him today, the weather felt more like an accomplice. On her way out of her apartment, she wrapped a scarf around her neck and pulled on a wool beanie to cover her messy hair, which she planned to keep on all day. Or for as long as she was in Noah's presence.

"Your nose is red."

She imagined that most guys would have taken an observation like that as a sign to head back inside, but Noah just winked. "Call me Rudy," she replied.

He quirked an eyebrow, then grinned. "Rudolph. Got it." After a pause, "Walk with me?"

They trudged along in the sand, watching waves curl onto the shore, leaving foamy remnants behind. Funny how they could be shoeless one night on this stretch of the coast but have to ward off frostbite only a few days later.

Okay, maybe that was being dramatic. Truth was, it

didn't take all that long for her to warm up and remove her scarf. That beanie would be staying put, though.

With each roll of a wave, Trace chased away the realization that moments like these were more fleeting than usual. Their charade was beginning to feel less and less like make-believe with each passing moment and Trace's unspoken fears of feeling left out were slowly being replaced with a new fear: How will she take it when Noah checks out of the inn for good?

"Any more thefts lately?"

His question startled her. Huh. She must've been preoccupied to not have obsessed over the inn during the last twenty-four hours. "Come to think of it, yes," she said. "Loretta sent an email out to staff that a rain shower head was missing among other things from the penthouse suite."

"Wow. So these criminals have tools."

"Apparently."

"Well, I bet the owners are paying attention now."

"Hm?"

Noah brushed her shoulder with his hand. "Lost in thought?"

She sighed and gave her head a shake. "Sorry, I guess it's being out here so early. It's knocked me out of my routine."

"I was just saying that the owners of the inn must be growing concerned about the theft. A shower head. That's brazen."

Trace squinted, her mind refocusing. "You're right. Up until now, I've wondered who was doing the stealing, but now I'm wondering how they're doing it. It's one thing to stuff a towel into a suitcase, but Loretta told me one of the inn's framed insignias was missing too."

"That's too bad."

"I'll say."

They walked along in silence, each engrossed in their thoughts. Noah broke the quiet. "What had your mind occupied back there?"

"So, so much. You wouldn't be interested."

"Hit me."

"Well, okay. I have some decisions to make about my future ... that job offer I told you about. So much to consider it's beginning to hurt my head, it's like I'm running in place with no end in view."

"And it's tiring."

"It is. I could start fresh with the new position I've been offered, but what if I end up doing the same thing? Still living in the same two-bedroom, one-bath apartment, still working hours I don't like, still ..." She let her words trail away, not wanting to sound overly pathetic. But if she were to keep talking out loud, she might add *still alone*. Not just alone in the couple sense, though it would be downright magical to have a man to be groggy with first thing in the morning. But not just that. She wanted to feel a part of things—not just some afterthought. Would changing jobs give her that chance?

He turned, his gaze brushing over her face, lingering there. "What do you think you'll do?"

She stopped. Such a simple question, yet no one in her life—not her mother, nor father, nor friends, even—got personal with her very often, if at all. And yet here was

Noah, asking her about something she cared about, like he cared.

Best pretend boyfriend she'd ever had.

"I'm not sure."

He took her hand briefly, then as if noting her surprise, he gently let it go. "Then you're not ready. If you still have time, why not take it?"

She nodded and smiled. Trace didn't yet know what decision to make, but a new kind of contentment settled in her heart. And, for right now, all she wanted to do was lean into that.

And maybe ... have Noah hold her hand again.

Every part of her had warmed up except her hands. In hindsight, she should have brought mittens. True, she would have had to endure laughter from East coast travelers who deemed California weather, even the blustery December kind, as "perfect." But Trace would take comfort over their scorn any day.

He had walked with her up to the hotel's path, the one that overlooked the sea. Trace turned a look over her shoulder. "I suppose you're headed to work now."

"Just a few calls to make today. No meetings. Supply delays are killing me, but hopefully, I'll get some good news."

So that means you're free to spend most of the day with me, right?

She didn't say this out loud, of course. But now that

Noah had gotten her up and out early, didn't he owe her some kind of non-interrupted attention?

Again, she didn't utter a peep.

"I have an idea," he said.

She gave him the most nonchalant glance she could muster.

He gestured with a flick of his head. "It's that tree in there." They were standing outside the chapel now and Noah pointed at the sad little tree by the window, the one that the maintenance staff had dragged inside as an afterthought.

"The Charlie Brown one?"

"Exactly!" He grinned. "Knew I could count on you to recognize its hopelessness."

"It's been on my list to get in there and toss some tinsel on it. Maybe string some new lights. I guess the guys didn't plug the lights in before wrapping the string around the branches. Many of them burned out already."

"Pathetic."

"Yeah!"

He laughed, then gave her a lopsided grin. "Let's do it then. Let's decorate that pathetic tree. Meet me tonight?"

Warm ... fuzzy ... she'd never quite had this feeling before but recognized it when it happened. A man, no—a gorgeous man—was inviting her for a clandestine tree trimming sesh in her favorite spot on this property. How could she say no?

"Um, okay."

He stepped closer, a grin on his face. His voice dipped. "You sound a little unsure."

She hummed a response.

"How can I convince you?" His gaze closed the gap between them, and Trace's knees nearly gave out. Every nerve ending stood at attention, announcing this was it ... Noah Bridges was about to kiss her right outside in front of everyone, well, in front of all those seagulls overhead.

His hand grazed her shoulder. She wanted to react in some way. Maybe even take charge. But all she could do was stare at the sober expression on his face, the hooded eyes staring back at hers, and lean into the magnetic draw of him, teetering between her independent spirit and the sudden desire to let go.

"Coming through!" Otis called out as he barreled toward them in a golf cart overladen with construction material.

Trace jumped back, as did Noah, until they were on opposite sides of the path. They watched in silence as Otis cut a swath between them, oblivious to what he had just interrupted. When Trace looked back at Noah, his eyes twinkled, but she saw a tinge of resignation in them too.

After setting up a time to meet Noah later, Trace wandered through the hotel's back entrance and into the cafe. A hot cup of coffee would help her parse through the feelings she'd been confronted with already this morning.

"Table for one?" the hostess asked.

Story of my life. Trace shook her head. "Actually, I'd like a cup of coffee to go." She thought a moment. "And if the soup of the day is ready, I'd like a bowl of that to take home too."

"You got it. I'll have someone bring you your coffee while I go back to check on the soup."

Trace spotted the inn owners as she waited. Sophia

gave her a demure wave, gesturing for her to come over. Trace took a deep breath and made her way across the cafe.

"Good morning, Trace," Sophia said.

Jackson, her brother, sat across from her, the table strewn with paperwork. She couldn't imagine having to decipher all those spreadsheets so early in the day. "Mornin', Trace. Having some breakfast before your shift?"

Trace clucked her tongue. "I hope you know I wouldn't show up to work dressed like this, boss."

Sophia laughed in that light way of hers. "Men are so clueless, aren't they?"

For his part, Jackson looked completely out of the loop.

"She's not working today," Sophia said, before looking up at Trace again. "I love your beanie. So chic."

"You don't mean it."

"Yes! I really do. Sometimes I miss back East and all the fun hats and boots and scarves that I wore on a daily basis."

"I suppose your time living in Italy was like that too?"

"Somewhat, yes. We had seasons there, too!"

Their laughter broke the ice.

"By the way, how is CJ?" Trace asked. CJ Capra, aka Christian Capra, was Sophia's husband and one of Trace's favorite fantasy writers. "I haven't seen him around here in forever."

"I've hardly seen him myself." Sophia dipped her chin, like she was sharing a secret. "He has been locked up in his writing cave for weeks. If I didn't remind him to eat, I'm not sure if he ever would!"

"Oh, I bet he's writing me something amazing. You

know I love reading everything he writes. Even if he has to grow a beard to do it."

Jackson snorted. "Chris is a big boy. I'm sure he can take care of himself."

Sophia and Trace turned a look on him.

He frowned, then light dawned on his face. "Oh, I get it. You weren't talking to me. My mistake. Carry on."

Jenny appeared as their laughter died away. "Here's your coffee." She handed the paper cup to Trace. "And I talked to Chef. It's a little early, but he's warming up a pot of yesterday's soup for you to take home. Hope that's okay. Should be ready in just a few more minutes."

"That's perfect. Something to look forward to at lunchtime."

"So if you're not working," Jackson said, "what're you doing here on your day off?"

Should she be telling her boss that she was here at daybreak to walk the beach with a hotel guest? Fortunately, she didn't have to answer that because Meg showed up. "Good morning, lovelies!"

Sigh. Meg was a morning person. One reason they could never be besties.

"I'm so glad to run into you, Trace," Meg said. "Didn't expect to see you here today."

If Trace weren't mistaken, she thought Meg caught eyes with Jackson ever-so-subtly. The hairs on her arms rose like a warning. "Just sipping some coffee and picking up lunch."

"Fabulous. That's just great. Um, could I talk to you for a sec?"

Trace tilted her head to the side. Sophia shifted in the

silence. Suddenly, Meg waved her clipboard as if what she was about to say was *no big deal.* "Whatever. I can just talk to you about it right here." She huffed a breath. "Well, it seems we have no one available to work the concierge desk on Christmas, and well, honey, the inn is packed. I really need you that day."

The moment was happening in slow motion. She had lamented being alone for the holidays. But spending her birthday with hundreds of hotel guests was not on her mind. Besides, a small part of her wondered if maybe, just maybe, Noah might want to spend the day with her.

Though he had not mentioned it. Yet, anyway.

"I, well ..." Trace took in Meg's hopeful expression, and the way Sophia held her breath, and the haphazard way Jackson was tapping the table with his pen. Fine. Whatever.

"Okay. I ... guess ... I can do that."

Meg pulled her into a hug. "You are wonderful! Thanks so much, Trace. You made my day!"

Jenny appeared and handed her a warm paper bag. "Soup's in there for you. Should I put this on your employee account?"

Sophia spoke. "It's on the house." She looked at Meg, who was grinning and nodding. "It's the least we could do."

With a quick nod of thanks, Trace hurried out of the cafe before they could snag her to wash the windows. Okay, so maybe that was dramatic. But still. She made a beeline for the front doors, sipping her coffee as she did.

Outside, those familiar bells reminded her heart that there were tougher things than having to work on Christmas. But when she reached into her pocket, she found nothing.

"Sorry, Hope. Didn't bring any money with me today."

"Oh, now, don't you worry about that. You have a nice day, now."

"You bet. This coffee will help." She laughed.

"What else you got in there?"

Trace glanced at the bag in her hand, nearly forgetting that she had picked up lunch. "Chef warmed up some of yesterday's soup for me."

Hope's smile faltered. She must have caught herself because she quickly smiled again, only this time, it seemed like overkill. If Trace weren't mistaken, there was a certain wistfulness in her eyes, a yearning. She followed Hope's gaze to the bag in her hand.

"Actually," Trace said, holding up the bag, "why don't you take this."

Hope shook her head. "Goodness, no. I couldn't."

As if a cloud fell away from her eyes, Trace took in the gloves Hope wore, tattered in spots. Her skin, where exposed, looked raw, and red, the effect startling. Trace gently pushed the bag into Hope's hand. "You would be doing me a favor. I'm not that hungry and I would hate for this food to go to waste."

Hope blinked rapidly. She nodded. "Well, then, we can't have that. If you're sure."

"No, we cannot, and yes, I am."

"Thank you, miss."

The contentment Trace felt earlier when she'd wandered into the cafe, before being drafted into working on Christmas, returned. And with a wave, she headed to her car, looking forward to the day—and night —ahead.

On the way into the hotel that evening, Trace pulled a wagon behind her with several boxes inside. She stopped and dropped a ten-dollar bill into the collection bucket.

"Thank you kindly, Trace!"

"You're still here," she said to Hope.

"I took another shift."

"But aren't your feet tired?"

"No ... I mean, not really. Thanks to your soup, I found a second wind."

Trace sensed Hope wasn't telling her everything. A flicker of something she couldn't quite put her finger on crossed in Hope's expression.

"Really. I am feeling fit as a fiddle tonight."

Trace laughed a little. "Well, all right then." She leaned in close, flicking a glance over her shoulder at the wagon behind her. "Don't tell anyone, but I'm meeting a certain hotel guest in the chapel to decorate a tree tonight."

Hope squeezed her shoulders together in delight. "Your secret is safe." She crossed her heart as if to prove it.

Minutes later, Trace found Noah in the chapel, already set up. He spotted the wagon and began to unload it. "So, your birthday," he was saying.

"You mean my milestone birthday?"

Noah put two heavy boxes onto a chapel pew. "Yes," he said, "that's the one. By the way, what's in these boxes —coal?"

"Ha-ha-ha."

"Don't you mean ho-ho-ho?"

Trace snorted, then covered her mouth as Noah coughed out a surprised laugh. Guess he hadn't spent much time with *real* women ...

"Now over here," Noah said, pointing to smaller boxes, "we've got ourselves dozens of candy canes."

Trace took in the boxes of small red-and-white-striped candy canes. "You planning to play Santa?"

"Good try, but no." He ripped open a box. "I thought we could decorate the tree with them, and then on Christmas, the hotel could give them out at the front desk or something."

Trace gaped at him. "You old softie!"

He shrugged. "Just an idea."

"Well, I like it. Now getting back to my fabulous contributions." She flipped open the top of a box. "I'll have you know these Christmas decorations are rare and anyone would be happy to display them on their tree."

"And you didn't use them yourself because ...?"

"Agatha." She sighed. "My cat would destroy them. She swats at anything within paw length."

"She sounds lethal."

"You don't know the half of it."

He quirked a grin. "Oh, almost forgot—I have one more contribution." He revealed a small drummer boy. "Had one like this as a kid so when I spotted it at a shop in the harbor, I picked one up."

"Aw, he's so sweet."

Noah flashed her a grin. "I think it gives the tree meaning, don't you?"

She studied him for a few seconds. Then nodded. "I agree."

"Anyway ... as I was saying. You mentioned you didn't have any plans for the big day, so let's make some. And not something cheesy, like a hot dog for dinner."

She waved a hand in front of her face. "That's all changed."

"What do you mean?"

She shrugged, not caring to talk about it. "I agreed to work on Christmas Day."

"You didn't."

"Really, it's not a big deal."

He dropped his fist to the top of a pew. "Well, I think it's a big deal."

"Why?"

"Because you mentioned it."

"No, why do you want to spend my birthday with me? Honestly, you've gone above and beyond to help me with this little charade already."

He frowned, and she noticed that the little dent between his eyes had deepened. She really wanted to know what that meant ... "You sick of me?" he asked.

"No!" She laughed self-consciously. "I just mean, well, look at you right now, decorating this tree—it's not even mine."

"Was my idea."

"True."

A pause settled between them. He stared at her, thoughts flickering across his face. Finally, he said, "So let's switch gears and go out on Christmas Eve."

A shimmy of chill ran through her, but she dared not meet his eyes.

When she didn't answer him, he continued. "So ... will you allow me to take you, my good friend, out to dinner on the eve of your birthday or not?"

My good friend? She licked her lips, nodding. "Why not?"

Noah's face split into a grin. "Great. Now hold this ladder for me while I get up there and fix those lights."

She did as asked, trying not to fixate on the way he wore those jeans. Was it hot in here? She fanned herself with her hand briefly. Who knew the smell of pine mixed with a man's smoky cedar-scented cologne could bring on so much heat?

"What do you think?"

Trace jerked a look up. "Ouch."

"You okay?"

"Um, neck spasm."

"Okay. So ... the lights. You can let go of the ladder now, by the way."

"Of course." She pried her hands off it and stepped back. "Wowza. That's way better. You're quite orderly, aren't you?"

He chuckled as he climbed down the ladder. "My mother would sure love to hear that said about me."

"Were you a messy boy?"

"I like to think of it as creative."

A couple of pine needles had adhered themselves to the lapel of Noah's shirt. Without a second thought, she reached out to brush them away. On contact, an unexpected, electric-like charge traversed her arm and she let out a tiny gasp. She tried to pull her hand back, but he caught it—and held it between them.

"I, uh, was just"—She worked to unscramble her thoughts for her words—"going to brush away some pine needles."

"Yeah?" His voice was questioning, and he didn't let go of her hand.

She bit her lip and peered up at him. "Was that too ... motherly? Personal? Familiar?"

A grin formed on his mouth. "For what?" He pulled her closer to him, narrowing the gap between them.

"For ... you know." She released a big sigh. "For what we're doing."

His voice went lower still. "Which is?"

The speed of Trace's heart increased. She blinked and took a breath to steady herself. This evening had taken a turn she hadn't seen coming. Was supposed to be a light-hearted Christmas tree-trimming party, right?

Yeah, right. She knew the precipice she was tiptoeing across this night—and so did he. Trace yanked her arm away. "Noah Bridges, stop teasing me right now. You know what I'm asking!"

He held up two hands, as if under arrest. "I'm not teasing, Trace. I promise."

Trace stuck her hands in her back pocket and walked over to the boxes she had brought from home. Though she had never told Noah the deep, dark secret that she had never had a boyfriend—her date to Priscilla and Wade's wedding didn't count!—she believed he knew. And, if so, teasing her like this was not nice. Not nice at all.

They needed to stick with the plan—*stick to the plan*

and nobody gets hurt! A rueful smile found her, and she began hunting through the Christmas items. She plucked a stuffed wise man from the box. Then two more.

"We should put these on the tree somewhere because what says Merry Christmas more than three wise men? I mean, these guys were looking for Jesus so they could give him gifts, and they traveled so far for so long following that big ol' star up in the sky that they deserve some recognition for that, am I right?"

"Trace?"

She kept her head down, still doing the work they had come here to do.

But Noah wouldn't allow that. Gently, he tipped her chin up with his finger. Noah's face reflected a tentative smile, as if doubt played a part in his thoughts.

No one knew doubt better than her.

Noah took each of the wise men out of her hands and sat them down on the pew. They fell into each other.

"Look, Noah, maybe this wasn't such a good idea. I mean, maybe Harry was right."

"Harry ... Styles?"

"Who? No, no." She shook her head. "I mean from the movie, 'When Harry Met Sally.' That's the premise—that men and women can't be friends. Well, maybe there's something to that."

"Hmm." He pressed his lips together, contemplation taking over his expression.

"I appreciate what you've done. Thomas hasn't been nearly as annoying as he usually is, and frankly, I feel ever more *seen*, lately. But ..."

"But?"

She hung her head, her gaze dusting the ground. "I don't know. Maybe"—she lifted her chin—"maybe we need to remember that this is all just pretend. And act accordingly."

He gazed at her for a beat. "What if I don't want it to be pretend?"

Chapter 6

Last Christmas

What if I don't want it to be pretend?

Trace had been replaying Noah's words in her mind for the past twenty-four hours. That's how long it had been since she had seen him. Even before he had dropped that statement on her, he'd told her he would be out of commission today. Something about driving to Los Angeles to meet with an artist. Still, she had stolen peeks of the lobby all day on the offhand that, for once, LA traffic had experienced a good day and he had returned early.

She should probably get some credit for this lost time without him.

Once that thought fully registered, Trace silently scolded herself to *get a life*. Despite what Noah had said, nothing had changed. She was still single, and he would still be checking out in a very short time.

"Oh my gosh, Trace? Was that you?" Liddy said, showing up without warning.

Trace frowned at her old concierge partner. Liddy's expressive face stared back at her.

"Well?"

"Girl," Trace said, "I have no idea what has you all lit up right now." She didn't want to add that Liddy had just pulled her out of a perfectly confusing daydream.

"Ha. Spot on terminology. I'm talking about the Christmas tree in the chapel. Saddest little thing I'd ever seen—and I told maintenance so—but you fixed it, didn't you?"

"Well ..."

Liddy's mouth curled into a smile. "You and that heart-throb who pulled you into his arms the other day did it." She was nodding now, her tongue stuck to her upper lip.

Trace rolled her eyes. "I put up with all that googly-eyed stuff when you were dating Beau. Don't make me go through that again."

"Don't blame me. You're the one inspiring all the 'goo-gly-eyed stuff' these days." She made air quotes around the words.

Every inch of Trace didn't want to admit this, but she missed this friendly banter with her old concierge mate. She wasn't sure what was going on to make Liddy so out of reach lately, but she wouldn't let the time go to waste.

"Fine. Whatever. Out of the kindness of that man's heart, yes, he helped me spruce up that embarrassment of a tree."

"Well." Liddy laid a hand on the counter before taking a surreptitious glance around. She lowered her voice and spoke fast. "Tell me the truth. You loved every minute of it."

Now, see, this was where Trace's natural inclination would be to tell Liddy, darling as she was, to mind her own beeswax. But isn't this what she'd been wanting? To feel part of something, even if it was a co-worker sticking her nose where it didn't belong?

"If you must know, loved might not be the right word, but"—she shrugged—"sure, we had a good time."

"Called it."

Trace laughed. "You did no such thing, Lid. Unless ... are you talking behind my back?" A flash of something Trace couldn't exactly explain—Surprise? Fear? Horror?—appeared on Liddy's face and just as quickly disappeared. Her eyes darted about briefly before refocusing on Trace. Her smile looked pasted on.

"The tree really is stunning." She took a few steps backward, as if leaving, but pointed at Trace. "You should get a bonus. I'm telling Meg!"

When she'd gone, Trace muttered, "Yeah, yeah. I'm not holding my breath ..."

"Excuse us?"

He was wearing a dark suit coat, a white shirt open at the collar. She wore a shiny, cream-colored number with a flat gold necklace, her highlighted hair in beach waves. Probably attending the wedding reception in the ballroom later today.

"How may I help you?"

The man spoke. "We were hoping to view a room for a future stay. Do you have any available that we could see?"

Trace glanced over to the front desk and frowned. No one there. She bit back a sigh. Sometimes she thought they all took breaks at the same time, especially since they knew she'd worked at the inn long enough to step behind their desk and do their jobs too.

Did that sound snippy?

She smiled and picked up the phone. "If you don't mind waiting, I will call housekeeping to see what is open and available right now."

"Wonderful," the woman said.

Quickly, Trace called, received the number of an empty room, then asked the couple to wait while she retrieved a key from the front desk. While there, she signaled for Thomas.

"Whaddaya need, beanie butt?"

"What is *wrong* with you?"

He laughed. When she tried to hand him the key, he stepped back and held up his palms. "I have a classic car to pull up. Sorry."

She glanced over at the couple patiently waiting at the desk. "If I leave, the lobby'll be empty."

He walked backward. "I'll make it quick for you, fish face. Tell 'em to go on up and I'll be right behind them. Number?"

"Two twenty."

He shot her with his pistol finger and jogged out the front door.

Back at the concierge desk, she said, "I'm sorry I don't have anyone to show you the room just yet—"

The man smiled. "That's not necessary." He reached for the key. "May I? We are on our way to a function and don't have much time to spare."

Trace hid a frown. It burned her to not provide top

service, but she couldn't do it all alone. She wicked a glance toward the front door and then back to the couple.

She nodded. "Of course. If you don't mind seeing yourself to the second floor, please take the elevators at the far end of the lobby. Thomas will join you momentarily to answer questions."

"Thank you," he said. "We will return the key promptly."

She spent the next fifteen minutes answering phone call after phone call, watching Thomas crisscross the lobby, and finally, seeing Hans show his face at the front desk, followed by Hannah. The Christmas streaming service had been stuck on an unending loop of "Silver Bells" and if she had to hear grown humans singing *ring-a-ling* one more time, she would lose her lunch.

She was about to say so when Hannah hung her purse over her shoulder and began to leave the front desk.

Trace marched over. "Uh-uh-uh. Where are you going?"

Hannah didn't move except to look Trace up and down. "Break."

"What do you call the past twenty minutes?"

"A meeting."

"You're kidding. On a Saturday? I've been holding down the fort alone."

Hannah narrowed her eyes. "What's gotten into you?"

Trace sputtered. She took a breath. Saying what she thought would earn her the reputation of chief pity-party thrower. This kind of situation had happened before when the inn was understaffed, but Trace usually shrugged and kept moving. Something told her she should raise some noise about the excessive meetings over at the front desk, but then again, how much longer would she even be here?

Better to leave on good terms, if that's what she decided to do.

"You know what? Enjoy your break. I'll take up the staffing issues with Hans."

Hannah screwed up her mouth. "Oo-kay."

The next two hours rolled by with little fanfare, though much activity. At some point, Thomas returned the key, stating that the couple had already toured the room by the time he got there. Stephanie had arrived in late afternoon to help at the concierge desk, and the two had been buzzing along, making event reservations and answering questions nearly non-stop.

At one point, she looked up from the desk, phone in her ear, to see Noah speeding through with his AirPods on, hands gesturing, mouth moving. He sent her a wink and that was the last she'd seen of him.

The days might be shorter this time of year, but hers never seemed to let up. The next time she glanced out the entry doors, the sun had set. Trace blew out a sigh.

Stephanie tapped her shoulder. "Looks like a lull is coming. Mind if I take a break before you leave for the night?"

Trace pushed away from the desk and stood. "Go for it. I'm going to stretch a little. Feel like I'm rolled tighter than a pumpkin loaf right now."

She almost didn't see the woman standing at the concierge desk, her red hair flowing down her shoulder in waves. "Good evening. How may I help you?"

"I, uh"— She glanced over at the front desk, empty again, then smiled at Trace. "Could you help me reach a guest?"

She'd already talked to Hans about the front desk's follies, but once again, her concerns were ignored. That was an issue for another time. Trace's fingertips hovered over her computer keyboard. "I will certainly try."

The woman put her purse onto the counter and slid out a compact mirror. A pen and other items fell out and she swiped them all back in. She flashed dark-lined eyes at Trace but said nothing. Instead, she opened up the compact and began making kissy lips in her reflection.

"The name?"

She smacked her ruby-red lips together and without looking away from the mirror said, "Bridges."

Trace's hands stilled. As in ...?

"Noah Bridges." The woman snapped the compact shut. "He's my fiancé but isn't answering his phone. I figured this little podunk area of the coast probably doesn't have very good reception." She giggled at her joke.

"Your fiancé?"

"Yes. Did you find him? I know he's staying here."

Trace stared at the screen, as if in concentration. Of course, she didn't need to look up Noah's room number. She had it seared onto her brain.

But he'd never mentioned anything about having a ... a ... fiancée. All he said in passing was that he'd been dumped. That wounded-heart vibe about him had made Noah hard to resist, unfortunately. She sneaked a glance at the preening redhead waiting for his room number and, unfortunately, saw a flash of the ring she wore on her left hand.

Obviously, Trace had misread the vibe she'd seen in Noah, the one he had perpetuated with his woe-is-me comment about being dumped. Instead of wounded heart, she should have recognized him as a two-timer, a player, a Casanova-wannabe ...

"Ma'am?"

"Hmm?" Trace jerked a look up at the woman with the gorgeous hair and nails waiting to rip her heart out, er, to get Noah's room number.

Trace reached for the phone. "It's customary to call the guest before giving out room numbers. One moment, please."

Noah answered on the second ring.

"Hello, Mr. Bridges. This is Trace at the concierge desk."

"Trace?" The laughter in his voice sent ice through her veins. "Why didn't you call my cell? And why the Mr.—"

"You have a guest at the front desk. A Ms."—Trace gaped at the woman, who quickly provided her name— "Ashley."

The tone of his voice changed to conspiratorial. "You're ... kidding."

"I am not."

Noah released a long, heavy sigh into the phone. He'd been caught and he knew it. Not that he owed her anything. It was all pretend anyway, well, except for what he said yesterday in the chapel about not wanting things to be pretend.

But they had not fleshed that out and now it had become obvious to Trace that all he meant by that was he didn't want the holidays to be over. He'd have to leave the inn to head back home and, well, there went the daily housekeeping service!

"Trace."

"What would you like me to say to your guest, sir?"

He groaned. "Fine. Send her up."

The lobby continued to surge and offer up a cacophony of sounds, a melding of tourists rushing about combined with the top ten songs of Christmas. She'd heard Michael Bublé croon in her ear so often that they were on a first-name basis. As the guests continued to rush here and there, Trace stood much like one of the tall wooden soldiers that flanked the ballroom, stony still, unable to make a move.

"What's that?" Stephanie said, pointing to an envelope on the counter.

Trace pulled her mind out of the fray. She picked up the envelope, noting the name written across the front in Noah's handwriting: *Ashley*.

"It's nothing," she said. "I'm leaving anyway, so I'll take care of it." She dug her purse out of a drawer, dropped the envelope inside, then walked out of the inn for the night.

So this is what an out-of-body experience felt like. Noah felt sure he was having one. It was the only way to explain the battle going on between his head and heart right now.

Ashley sat back on the couch, legs curled beneath her, eyes on him, like a bull to a red cape. He had hoped and prayed that this moment would come, but now that it was here? Noah wanted to shrug his shoulder and whisper, *Meh.*

His parents raised him to be a gentleman, though, so he knew better than to say that out loud. But what was she doing here? Why now?

"Can I get you something to drink?" He sprang up from the wingback chair, strode into the small kitchen, and flung open the fridge. "Uh, not a lot in here. Sparkling water? Juice?"

"That's the strongest you've got?"

He remembered the bottle of red wine that he had tucked into an upper cabinet, the one he'd been saving for something special. This wasn't it. He pulled out the fizzy water and shut the fridge door a little too hard.

"Sparkling water it is." He poured them each a glass and brought the drinks to the living area.

She stared into her glass but didn't sip, instead placing it on a coaster. Noah had remembered those wide eyes of hers differently. He'd been mesmerized by them in the past but couldn't exactly remember why now. Something had changed.

"What's brought you here, Ash?"

"Isn't it obvious?"

Tight red dress, Cheshire cat smile ... the ring on her finger. He darted a look at her eyes again. She raised her eyebrows, her smile the kind he'd dreamed of once. In a shot, she was off the couch and on his ... lap.

She giggled. "Boy, you are dumb, aren't you?" She was

running long-nailed fingers through his scalp. "I came here to accept."

He was the Tin Man, unable to think or move. With effort, he cleared his throat, hoping that would clear his head, too. "Accept?"

"Your proposal."

"My ... proposal."

"Yes, Noah. I'll marry you!"

Their noses were inches apart. He took in her eyes, her smile. Ashley Farrington had been everything he had wanted in a wife. She had dazzled him from the first time his mother introduced them in Maine.

But Ashley had turned him down. What had she said again? Oh, right. He was too ... boring and owned too many pairs of jeans ... and boots. She wanted her man in a well-fitted suit and monogrammed cufflinks.

He'd never even gotten the ring back from her.

Noah pressed his eyes shut, drawing sense back into his head. Gently, yet firmly, he moved Ashley off his lap. He stood. "Be serious."

"I want you in my life, Noah. I've never forgotten you, have dreamed about you over and over."

Her eyes looked brighter than he'd remembered them, with a feverish intensity to them. Though he once longed to hear that she dreamed about him, she was not the Ashley he knew. Something was up, but he wasn't about to try to put together this puzzle right now. Not with Trace downstairs, no doubt growing more upset with him by the second.

Noah shook his head. "It's over."

"What do you mean, over?" she sputtered.

"I mean, I no longer think we should be married, Ash."

She curled up her nose at him. "You have got to be kidding me."

"I wouldn't kid about something this serious."

"What are you saying? You kid about everything! I have never found that all too charming, Mister, but I dealt with it!"

He pressed his mouth shut, a quirk in his cheek, and nodded.

"Don't give me that know-it-all smile, Noah. I came all the way here from Maine. Do you realize that? And suddenly *you* don't want to marry *me*?" She shook her head, then leaned toward him, pointing a daggered finger at his chest. "You're the one who kept calling and texting—and you wrote me that letter!"

Noah swallowed, memories he had buried suddenly brought under a heat lamp. "I ... yeah. I did that, didn't I? But that was months ago."

"Surely your devotion didn't change in a few short months."

He lifted his chin. "Apparently, it did."

"I don't understand. *I'm* still the same person." She looked him up and down, her voice tinged with sarcasm. "And you haven't changed a bit."

That's where she was wrong. He *had* changed. She was beautiful, nothing new there, but now he wanted more than eye candy in his life. He wanted someone he could sense from across the room, even without knowing she was there. He wanted the kind of beauty that springs from who a woman is inside, not what she wears. And ... he wanted someone who could make him laugh like a hyena ... and vice-versa.

Noah crossed his arms, digging his heels into the carpet. "You have to go."

Ashley draped a hand on her hip. "Not until we figure this out."

"I'm sorry, Ash, but there's nothing to figure out. You told me months ago I was too boring—"

She rolled her eyes. "So sensitive you are! That's the artist in you. Really, Noah, you need to toughen up."

A mirthless grin grew on his face. He dropped his gaze to the ground. The dream he'd conjured last year involving Ashley had shattered, and he did not miss it. At all.

"You were right to turn me down, Ashley. I see that now." He sighed. "And I'm sorry you came all this way to hear that, but I've never been more sure about anything." He started to walk to the door.

"So that's it. Mr. Generous has decided to unceremoniously kick me out. After all I went through to get here."

"Not at all." Noah opened the closet door and retrieved an extra blanket and pillow. "For tonight, the place is yours. I'll find somewhere else to sleep, but I want you gone by morning. Goodbye, Ashley."

By the time he reached the first floor, Noah realized his error. He had a pillow and a blanket under one arm and nowhere to go. Kind of like that time he ran away from home after his father wouldn't let him have a third scoop of ice cream. Only back then, he could turn tail and be home by bedtime.

He groaned and snapped a look down the long hall toward the front desk. Dicey. Staff was getting to know him around here. Why open himself up to probing questions when he still hadn't had a chance to talk to Trace?

Man ...Trace. He already knew by the icy phone call, she was upset. Surely he could smooth things over with her tomorrow.

But for now, sleep. He darted toward the glass doors and headed outside, the cool night air popping a hard one to his chin. Great. Light caught his eye. The chapel was lit up, much like the night he checked in. The night he met Trace.

He tromped over through the wet grass and peered into a window. Empty. Also like that night. With a glance around, Noah tried the door, and when he found it open, he hurried inside.

Trace may have walked out of the inn looking cool as a you-know-what, but underneath it all, she seethed. "Everything okay?" Hope asked her.

She dropped a dollar into the bucket, barely able to speak. Still, she nodded before jogging to her car.

"I'll say a prayer for ya," Hope called after her.

At home in her apartment, Trace plopped Agatha onto her lap and began stroking her white fur.

"You know, he could've told me to send her packing, but did he? No. He said to send her up! I can't wait to see her!"

Agatha twisted a doubtful look at Trace, who frowned in response. "Well, you weren't there. He may not have said all that, but he might as well have. I could hear it in his voice."

When Agatha didn't respond, Trace sighed, grateful to be in the quiet of her own home. The day had overwhelmed her and made it difficult to think about decisions she needed to make soon, let alone dwell on a precarious relationship with a fake boyfriend. Sam had left messages two days in a row, requesting an answer from her about the job offer.

"All this is probably for the best," she said. Trace's first impression of Noah Bridges was right: too hot to handle. He's probably more comfortable with a woman on each arm than he is about committing to just one. Why would she think otherwise?

Agatha tried to slink away, but Trace doubled down on the petting action. "Such a sweetheart you are, consoling me this way. What would I do without you?"

Agatha let loose a shrill *meow,* then hopped off Trace's lap and pranced away.

The thought occurred to Trace that she could possibly, maybe be overreacting. Just a tiny bit. She bit the inside of her lip. That woman was probably messing with her. Noah never said anything about having a fiancée in his life or about proposing to anybody. That ring was probably fake, something she flashed around to feel good about herself.

Or maybe that was petty. *Meow.*

Trace grimaced. She had been avoiding the letter all night, embarrassed that she had not only stolen it from the concierge desk, but done so in public. Security would prob-ably confront her tomorrow and she'd be faced with fessing up or taking the fifth. Either way, they'd proclaim: Guilty!

The temptation proved too much, and Trace pulled the letter out of its envelope and unfolded it on her lap. From the first word, she cringed. Such a voyeur, she was! Still, she fell headlong into reading the words written in Noah's handwriting:

Ash,

I haven't been able to stop thinking of you. I miss you and have dwelled long and hard on everything you said to me after my proposal. I am taking it to heart, Ashley. All of it. And I hope that you will give me another chance to prove my worth to you.

From the day we met, I couldn't help but think that there would be something special between us. I am still holding out hope that you too, after some reflection, will feel the same way.

I love you and know you need some time, so I am offering that to you with this promise: When you are ready, I'll be here for you.

Always,
Noah

A thick knot at the base of her throat made it difficult for Trace to swallow, but a few hot tears exited her eyes anyway. Any embarrassment she'd felt over reading his private letter dissipated. Noah loved the woman enough to propose, enough to pen a love letter and beg her to come back to him. Worse, he had made her a promise that he would wait for her.

Trace had warned herself. *Don't. Fall. In. Love.* But had she listened? Sadly, no. She had been his momentary stand-in, his game to play while Ashley made up her mind to fall back into his arms. And by the looks of things, she had done just that. Game over.

Trace sat in silence for a good long while, replaying her regrets. There were many, and not just from recent times. She brushed her gaze around the room, grateful for what she had—her home, a Christmas tree bursting with memories, and Agatha, snotty as she could be sometimes. But there had to be something more. Had to be.

Trace grabbed her phone and began scrolling through her messages. One from her father, another from her stepmom, one from Noah—she wouldn't be listening to that one—and a message from Sam. Had she made up her mind yet? When could she start?

Trace sank into her couch, thinking about that last Saturday she worked when chaos ensued. She had come home so tired that night, and frankly, shifts like that were getting old. If she were going to be run ragged at work, she might as well do it with a raise and a management title.

Besides, a change would do her good. No more working with people who probably wouldn't miss her anyway, and bonus, she wouldn't be subjected to looking around the inn's lobby every day just to be reminded of the one who, in a very short time, had both captivated and broken her heart.

Trace would not admit that to anyone but herself, but it was true. She had violated her own warning and now was paying the price.

With resolve, Trace picked up the phone and rang Sam Chambers to give him the news.

Chapter 7

Blue Christmas

"Saw your boyfriend sleeping in the chapel last night."

"Oh?" Trace kept her eyes on the computer screen. She only had an hour to confirm all twenty-five golf reservations for tomorrow before she would be heading out the door to meet with Sam.

"None of my business, but I sure hate to see a grown man chased out of his own room."

"Uh-huh." Twenty-two reservations confirmed ...

Hans turned to stare over the top of her computer screen. He leaned onto his elbow and grinned as innocently as a toddler with a handful of markers. "You wouldn't know anything about that, would you?"

"One more to go ..."

"I would hate to have to tell Mr. Riley that one of his guests had been purposely locked out of his room, and that the poor man was left to spend the night sleeping against the hard back of a pillow-less pew."

Trace peeled a look up and narrowed her eyes. Noah slept in the chapel? She cleared her throat and handed Hans a clipboard. "Here's your cheat sheet. Your guys are going to want to be ready to load the van with twenty-plus sets of clubs throughout the morning."

He took the clipboard without looking at it. "So, as I was saying—"

"Clean up on aisle five!" Thomas shouted, running through the lobby with a maintenance guy on his heels. "Clean up on aisle five!"

"You get back here!" Hans hollered after him.

Thomas did a one-eighty and jogged backward. "Can't! The chapel needs all hands on deck!"

Trace and Hans frowned at each other. Trace slid a look at Stephanie. "You okay to watch the desk?"

"Yes, ma'am."

Another thing to look forward to with a looming birthday—the younger generation thinking it's perfectly fine to call a thirty-something woman *ma'am*.

Running wasn't her thing, but walking real fast, that she could do. Trace nearly skidded down the hall, but as she turned the corner, about to push open the glass door to the chapel lawn, she slowed.

The only real reason she followed Thomas to the chapel like a mama bear rounding up cubs right now was ... Noah. Did the clean-up have anything to do with him? Would she find him there, red lipstick smeared all over his manly face? What would he say to her?

And the biggest question of all: Would Ashley be curled up with him beside the tree that she and Noah had painstakingly decorated together?

Gross.

She shoved open the door and stepped into the cool air, but instead of making her way to the chapel, she walked to the edge of the path overlooking the gray-blue sea. She breathed in an abundance of salt air noting how the weather had see-sawed lately. While the past couple of days had been rather drizzly and opaque, today the sun tried to make an appearance behind fat splotches of clouds.

Trace blew out a long breath. She didn't need to get involved. Now was the time to start stepping back to let others do what she usually did: jump into the fray.

Decision made, Tracy was ready to pivot and go back inside when a commotion at the chapel caught her attention. Loretta was pacing on the lawn and squawking into a phone. "I need some of that chalk! And a shop vac. And bring me buckets and rags, lots of buckets and rags!"

A trickle of fear slithered through Trace's insides creating a sickening twist in her gut. Curse those mystery novels she read as a child! With a big, hot sigh she changed directions once again and headed toward Loretta, who was off the phone now and wringing her hands until they were crimson.

"What's wrong, Loretta?"

The woman swung around and spiked her fingers in the air. "Ants!"

"Excuse me?"

"Some numbskull put candy canes all over that tree in there and now the chapel is crawling with itty bitty ants!" She shuddered like she was shaking the heebie-jeebies right out of her, then gave Trace the stink eye. "I hate them."

Oh, dear. Trace sneaked a look at the chapel doors, open wide. "I'll go see if I can help."

Once inside, she found Noah bent over and yanking the tree out by its top branch. The cut tree appeared to be moving in one fluid motion, like a jellyfish stretching and contracting to propel itself forward. On closer inspection, those movements were made up of tiny moving trails, pathways filled with thousands and thousands of ants. The entire thing reminded her of the intersection of the 101 and 405 freeways in Los Angeles during rush hour.

She began to itch.

Noah wore a scowl for the history books. "Guess the candy canes weren't the brightest idea."

She almost felt sorry for him, looking all disheveled and discouraged, with pine needles sticking to his bedhead. Almost.

Trace plucked one of the candy canes from the tree with her fingertips and shook it like a thermometer, trying to dislodge the cluster of ants. "I thought we left them wrapped."

He shrugged. "Looks like some kids got in during the day and thought it would be more *festive* to unwrap them."

She gaped at him. "*All* of them?"

"Every last one."

She frowned. "Super gross."

A cleaning crew arrived and began sweeping and sanitizing the chapel. If memory served her, a small recommittal ceremony would be held in there later tonight.

Trace smacked her hands together in a swiping motion and followed the ant-laden tree outside, where a maintenance guy wearing a hard hat and holding a chainsaw looked all too eager to power up the thing. *Run little ants,* she thought, *run!*

"We need to talk," Noah said. The small, dark bags beneath his eyes told her he hadn't slept all that well last night either.

She swung a look back to the lawn, where a group of swarthy maintenance guys had gathered around the guy with the chainsaw, all suited up for the occasion. You'd think the chapel was about to get a second story added to it. More excitement than these guys had seen in months, apparently.

"Can't." She peeked at the time on her phone. "I have an appointment. Goodbye, Noah." Then she spun around and headed toward the hotel parking lot.

The contract seemed to cover everything. Sam was offering her a raise, a title, and healthcare comparable to what she had at Sea Glass Inn. All she needed to do was sign.

"Everything look good to you, Miss Murphy?"

Sam's fatherly smile warmed her. She was making the right decision. She was sure, or at least, as sure as she felt she could be.

Trace nodded. "It does. Except it doesn't say exactly when you would like me to start." She had been surprised at the disarray when she stepped onto the property. Construction workers in every corner, with tarps and scaffolding a major distraction. The possibilities pulled her emotions in opposite directions. On the one hand, the boutique property could, finally, become a major contender along the coast. How exciting to be part of something like this!

By the looks of things, though, a lot more work needed to be done before that could happen. It was going to take an avalanche of effort to make guests comfortable during what appeared to be a lengthy transition time.

Sam watched her with an expectant face. Despite all the upheaval around her, Trace felt ready to make a change. She picked up the pen and signed.

Her new boss clapped his hands together. "Wonderful!" He swung a look behind him. "Joe!"

A man in paint-splattered clothes and a hard hat appeared. He handed a hard hat to her. "Here to give you a tour," he said. "Name's Joe."

"Oh?" She looked at Sam.

"Go on now. Joe will show you around while I have my assistant make copies and email these to you."

Trace followed Joe, watching as he pointed to stripped walls that would soon be plastered over and plastic-covered windows in varying shapes. "New front desk will be over this way." He gestured to an open area.

"Where are guests checking in now?"

He puckered his mouth a moment. "None of those on the property right now. Wouldn't be safe."

"I ... see." Uncomfortable warmth hit her cheeks. Had she even asked about current occupancy? And why not? Had she done her due diligence before signing her promise to commit to this job?

"'Course, when January comes 'round, if the desk's not ready, we can set up a table right over there." He gestured again to the empty area.

"So you do hope to open fully by January?"

"Have to, no matter what shape we're in."

She eyed him, then the open spot, trying to picture checking people in at a long card table.

"Wanna take the rest of the tour?"

She startled. "Yes. Please."

She followed Joe outside to a large outdoor courtyard with a lawn, a westward-facing viewing deck, and ... was that a chapel? She took in the small building, about half the size of the chapel at Sea Glass Inn, but otherwise, very similar in style. At least from what she could make out with all that draping around it.

"Trace?"

She spun around at the familiar voice, her heart behaving erratically. Noah stood behind her, his brows dipping low, his loam-colored waves sticking out of the bottom of his hard hat. "What are you doing here?"

"I could ask you the same."

She huffed a sigh now, getting her bearings. She wasn't talking to him right now, remember? Trace swung a quick look to the blue sea, drawing strength from it, before returning her gaze to him. "Are you following me?"

He cracked her a smile and she wanted to smack him for it. But how would that look to her new boss if he were to see it?

Probably not the best idea. And yet, what *was* he doing here?

He broke into her confusion. "This is the project I've been working on for the past couple of weeks. Longer than that, actually."

Are you kidding ...?

He crossed his arms and rooted his boots to the ground. "So maybe I'm the one being followed."

She scoffed. "Right." Something didn't feel right about this. "Why were you keeping your work here a secret from me?

"No secrets from me ..." He slammed his mouth shut, as if realizing just how ludicrous that sounded coming from him right now. He swallowed. "I mean, I didn't mean to keep you in the dark about my work here. It just never came up."

"Yeah, like your fiancée never came up." The words flew out of her mouth like a canary sprung from her cage. Trace wanted to fly after them with a butterfly net, but it was too late.

Noah reached out to touch her on the arm. She retracted it, leaving his hand flailing in the wind. "Trace," he whispered.

Joe raised an eyebrow but waited. She wasn't sure if he was taking things in so he could tell the boys at the water cooler all about it later or if he was simply confused.

Probably the latter.

"I'm sorry I let that out. Just a momentary lapse in judgment," she said. "I meant what I said earlier. I'm not interested in talking about this right now."

"You never said why you were here, taking a tour."

She bit back a retort. This was where she should tell him it wasn't any of his business why she was here, but the softness in his voice kept her from unleashing any of that. Trace wished she could turn back the clock a few days to when they were walking on the beach early in the morning, as if neither had a bother in the world.

"I've decided to accept the position I've been offered. I start in January, right after the holidays."

"Here?" Noah frowned. He raised his eyes to meet Joe's, then returned his gaze to her.

Trace scowled. Her temples began to throb. "Yes, here." She looked to Joe. "I've seen enough for today. Thank you for the tour, but I need to go now. I'll come back another day to finish it."

Wordlessly, Joe reached out his hand. She tilted her head and gave him a questioning look.

He pointed at her head. "The hat?"

She flipped a look upward. "Right." Trace removed the hard hat and handed it to him before walking away.

"Trace."

She turned around and held up her palm like a stop sign. "Something's not right here, Noah. I can feel it in my gut, though I'm not sure why."

He took a step forward. "I want to tell you about last night."

"Uh, no, thank you!" She pressed her fingers to her temple.

He leaned over her, concern in his voice. "You all right?"

She squeezed her eyes shut. "No. I have a headache."

"I'll get you some water."

She lifted her chin, half-closing her eyes against the pierce of the sun. "Is Sam building a chapel here?"

Noah blinked.

"It's not a hard question."

He gave her a little shrug. "Yeah. That's part of the plans."

"How long have you known about this?"

"Why does that matter?"

"Doesn't it strike you as odd?"

Noah glanced around and shrugged. "Not really. He said something about honoring an old friendship. I'm not all that involved. What I do know is that this job is very behind schedule and the money is going to be lost if we don't get to a certain point by end of the year."

"Are you serious?"

"Unfortunately, I am."

"I just committed to a new position here! What if it all falls apart?"

"Then you'll start fresh."

"What?" He had to be joking. "Whatever makes you think that would ever be good advice?"

The soberness in Noah's expression held her captive, which only infuriated her. "For one, you are one of the most honest people I've ever met, but for another, you let that hotel walk all over you."

"Really. Wow. You hardly know me!"

"I know what I've seen. You're so riddled with worry that a thirty-sixth birthday is practically a death sentence."

Tears threatened to overtake her, but she wouldn't let them. She shook her head, her jaw tightening. "Oh, no, you don't. Don't you try to ... to analyze me. What are you hiding from, huh?"

"What's that supposed to mean?"

"You told me you were staying at a hotel, at Christmas-time, all because your mother had the audacity to want you to be happy! Oh, wow, that's some sick threat now, isn't it? Poor you!"

Noah scoffed.

She stepped up to him, her face near his now. "It's more than that, though, isn't it? You made a commitment to someone and now that she's come to find you, you don't know what to do about it. Is that right?"

"No."

"Well, at least you have people in your life who care enough to meddle in your love life or come after you because they want to spend time with you!"

Noah reached out and gently rubbed the fleshy part of her upper arm. She wanted to lean into his warm touch, to revel in the way he soothed her with the simplest of actions.

"Trace."

She jerked away from him. "You know what? No. I don't care to do this right now."

He kept his eyes on her. "That's your right, but you're the one walking away, Trace. Not me."

"Sure—because I'm not giving you the chance to do it first."

"C'mon ..."

She shook her head, taking a step backward. As far as Trace knew, Noah's fiancée was still up in his hotel room, waiting to play house when he came home from a long day at the office. She shuddered at the thought. "I have to get out of here." Trace turned around and began to jog to her car.

"Wait," Noah called after her. "Let me drive you back. We need to talk more about this."

But Trace didn't turn again. She couldn't. Because she didn't want him to see that the floodgate holding back the wall of emotion in her heart had broken free, and all he'd see was a mess of tears flowing down her cheeks.

"You have to go." Noah was standing inside the doorway of the Florence suite, taken aback by the looks of the place. Ashley hadn't brought much with her, but in the brief time since she'd arrived, she had made herself at home.

The dining table had been moved to the other side of the kitchen, and two wingback chairs were now in its place. She had moved several paintings around and put a vase of flowers—they looked handpicked but from where he didn't know—on the island. He glanced inside the open closet to find his jeans, each paired with a T-shirt, all hanging in a neat row.

"I've been waiting all day to talk to you. Come." She patted the couch. "Sit next to me."

He used to admire Ashley's persistence. She had used that skill to find them seats in sold-out shows and coveted parking spots when he might have circled for a while longer. Back then, he marveled at her tenacity and her wit. She could lean out a car window and compliment a woman on her shoes—only to happen upon the same woman at her place of business and score a discount.

But now he realized there was always a catch.

So. What was her agenda now?

With the chairs gone, Noah took a seat on the couch. Ashley leaned toward him and sighed. "I forgive you."

"For?"

"Abandoning me last night after I traveled all this way."

He leaned forward, resting his elbow on his thighs. She couldn't hold onto him using those means. Not anymore. "Why did you come here?"

"What do you mean?" Her expression of surprise looked put on. Had she practiced that in the mirror? "I came here to accept your marriage proposal."

He quirked a rueful smile. "You could've called."

"I was hoping to see you for Christmas, baby, but then your mother told me you had decided not to come home." She trailed her fingernail down his shoulder. "So I had no other choice but to come after you myself."

"But why the sudden change of heart?"

"Not so sudden."

"Really." It wasn't a question.

"Of course, really. I re-read your letter and knew that I had made a terrible mistake."

A small part of Noah wished he had never penned that letter. He had not expected her to turn down his proposal. Hadn't occurred to him that she would. In a way, her turning him down a second time, even after he wrote her a letter, told him everything he needed to know.

Still, he had pined for her. Even when he checked into the Sea Glass Inn, his thoughts still went back to her. To them. If they had married, she might have come with him.

But then ... Trace. He'd been hooked by her prying questions and self-effacing ways, and when he'd noticed her being mistreated, a protective instinct rose within him. She should have slapped him when he'd pulled her into his arms like that. He knew this. But she had leaned into him, and though they had pretended that what had formed between them was fake, he knew better.

Something was there. And now he may have lost any chance to discover how real it could become.

But he wasn't going down without a fight. Especially now that he knew the truth about Ashley—from his mother, no less.

"You didn't make a terrible mistake when you turned me down, Ashley. You did me a favor."

"Excuse me?"

"I know about the lost trust fund."

She gasped. Her face turned a dark shade of red, darker than that dressed-to-kill number she waltzed into his hotel room wearing last night.

"You know, I never was a rich man. I'm not one now. But I would've given you the world to the best of my ability." He exhaled, regrouping. "You weren't interested in that, though. Or in me, really. Not until you blew through your money and had nowhere else to turn."

She glared at him.

"It's true, isn't it?"

When Ashley continued to stare him down, Noah stood and reached into his back pocket. He handed her a slip of paper, pivoted on his boot, and walked slowly to the door.

She looked from the paper to him, lifting one brow considerably. "A boarding pass?"

"You forget—my mother used to be a travel agent." He opened the door to the suite. "A car is waiting downstairs to take you to the airport."

Ashley opened her mouth in protest, but she must have

seen the finality in his expression because she set her jaw and approached him. When their faces were inches apart, she paused. "You know what? You used to be a gentleman." She flipped her hair over her shoulder. "It's obvious that I'm the winner here."

Chapter 8

Christmas (Baby, Please Come Home)

Trace couldn't help herself—she felt the losses. All the happy faces traversing the lobby right now weren't helping. She knew it was better to give than to receive, but her well had dried up. She didn't know how much more she had left to give.

"You okay, hon?" Priscilla appeared beside the concierge desk. "You seem out of sorts."

"Well, that's one way to put it."

Priscilla's smile probed. "How can I help you?"

Trace wasn't the crying type, but that's all she felt like doing right now. She fought against giving in to the tsunami on its way.

"Oh, dear." Priscilla flicked a look behind Trace. "Steph? Think you can handle the desk for the rest of the afternoon? I have an opening and my friend Trace here would like to take it."

"Sure thing."

Trace sputtered and touched the back of her head with her fingertips. "Is my hair a mess?"

Priscilla gestured toward the spa with a flick of her beautiful red tresses. "Come on." She leaned toward Trace as they strolled through the lobby. "It's not about the hair sometimes."

Even though the inn offered her a discount, Trace had never taken them up on it. Her hair, thin and wispy, did fine with a cut from a discount salon about every quarter. Priscilla led her to a cushioned seat and lofted a large cape over her.

"What's that smell?" Trace asked.

Priscilla stood behind her now, looking at her through the grand, lighted mirror. "Essential oils, darling. Right now I have sweet orange and lemongrass filtering through the air. Isn't it lovely?"

Emotion caught in her throat. Priscilla always was one of her favorites around here, even though they'd only met a few years ago. Always so positive, and giving, and here she was, taking Trace's mess of a life and offering it some love.

As if sensing Trace's inability to speak, Priscilla began brushing her hair out with long luxurious strokes. After a moment, she placed her hands on Trace's shoulders and softly said, "Let's shampoo you. I have just the thing."

It was like no other shampoo she'd ever had. Priscilla hummed while she worked, calling out hellos to other stylists and guests as they passed by inside the small salon. After rinsing out the shampoo, she massaged in conditioner with something that tingled and smelled like eucalyptus.

Back in her chair, Trace wondered if she would be able

to stay awake for a full haircut. Sweet relaxation had found her, and it came in like an unrelenting winter storm.

"May I do whatever I want?" Priscilla asked.

"Sure. Yes. Do."

Priscilla laughed. "Wow. Not sure I've ever been given such carte blanche before, but I am here for it."

Trace mustered a smile, but even she could see it was a weak one. Priscilla could have taken an electric razor to her head, and she probably would have just shrugged and pulled her beanie on over it. She had lost her oomph and didn't know what to do about it. She let her eyes loll shut.

After a while, Priscilla's voice cut through her melancholy. "Would you like to tell me what's been bothering you, hon?"

Trace peeled an eye open. Priscilla stared at her through the mirror again. The chair on either side of hers was empty. She inhaled and released a breath.

"I ..."

Priscilla's concern was evident, but she kept snipping.

"I don't know where to begin."

"It's about the man, isn't it? The one who looks like he just walked out of a rock-climbing catalog?"

"That obvious?"

"You seem, how should I say this, forlorn."

Trace licked her lips. "There's, uh, a lot going on right now." This was true, of course, but there was also a lot *not* going on right now too. She feared that if she were to begin to tell her tale of sadness, it would steamroll into one big crying session.

"May I offer my thoughts?"

"One of us should."

She laughed. "It's okay if you're not ready to talk—I can do that for the both of us just fine!" Priscilla sighed, and snipped, texturizing the ends of Trace's locks.

Trace stifled a tiny yawn. "It's just ... very complicated."

"Are you still seeing each other?"

Trace thought about that. She prided herself on her honesty but wasn't about to admit the silly alliance she and Noah had formed. She reasoned that in a short time, they had progressed beyond their ruse, so it would be okay to answer Priscilla's question. If it had been up to her, they would have kept that progression going.

But maybe even that was all in her head. Finally, she said, "He, uh, appears to have someone else in his life."

"Rats."

"I should have known."

"How would you know that if he didn't tell you?" Priscilla's shears sliced the air.

Trace made a face. She gestured to herself in the mirror.

Priscilla gasped and pointed those shears right at her, well, right at the mirror. "Don't you dare say what I think you're saying."

"You said yourself that Noah belongs in a catalog of rugged men." She shrugged. "Seriously, what would he want with someone like me?"

"Trace Murphy, you are gorgeous, inside and out."

Trace grimaced.

Priscilla stopped what she was doing and put her tools on a tray. She turned Trace's chair around and bent so low that they were face to face. She had seen Priscilla do the same thing with her daughter, Amber. "You are a gorgeous woman worthy of love. Now, I don't want to hear one more whisper of criticism from you."

Trace mulled Priscilla's admonishment, vaguely noticing the change in her hair. Even wet, it appeared to have more volume.

Priscilla picked up her shears again. "Love is hard, Trace. It's confusing. As you know, my first relationship didn't work out."

"I remember that guy coming to the inn and trying to win you back."

"Ah, but it only looked that way. Truthfully, he was using me. I was his easy way out."

"Yeah." Trace thought about that. "How did you stay strong and not give in?"

"By then, I knew myself. And I thought I deserved better."

"I'm not really into all that self-help stuff. No offense."

Priscilla smiled in a non-offended way. She stopped and put a hand on Trace's shoulder. "Me neither! But it goes deeper than that. We love hard, and sometimes that means our hearts are left vulnerable. We can either stay beaten down or realize that we're made for more."

Trace waited. They caught eyes in the mirror. Priscilla was smiling now. "I'm talking about faith, girlfriend. Look around for a moment."

Trace took in the beautifully appointed spa, the high-end sconces, and draped walls. The tower of products on an antique table. This spa had been a vision of the Riley siblings and every detail had been planned out.

"As beautiful as all this is, it's temporary. The Lord

says that a good name is far better than riches. You, my friend, have a very good name."

"Ha. I don't know about that. Lately, I've been wondering if I've been too focused on work when maybe I ought to be more focused on just being a better person."

Priscilla's gaze darkened. "Who you are is already woven into the fabric of your life. I've seen your generous heart myself. I'm not saying that we all aren't due a little self-reflection at times, but my word, Trace, please don't be so hard on yourself."

Tears welled behind Trace's eyes. She thought about the pity party she'd thrown heading into this month. How she felt forgotten and unseen. How any tiny bit of atten-tion—a job offer, a hot guest showing her some attention—pumped her up in a way she'd never felt before, in a way she needed.

She lowered her voice. "I have a secret."

Priscilla's brow dipped. "That doesn't sound good."

"It is to me." She watched Priscilla's expression change as she continued to shape her hair. "It's confidential."

Priscilla caught eyes with her in the mirror. "Well, then, it doesn't go past me."

"I'm leaving."

"Leaving, as in ...?"

"Sea Glass Inn. I've been offered a position somewhere else."

Priscilla froze, holding her shears above Trace's head. Slowly, she began moving them again. "Does Jackson know? Or Meg?"

Trace screwed up her face. "I was planning to give my notice today."

Priscilla raised a brow.

"When I got up the courage."

"Well, darling, I don't know how we're going to get along without our heartbeat. That's how I think about you."

Trace laughed, but tears sprang from her eyes. "You're too kind."

Their conversation died away as Priscilla dried Trace's hair, bringing more style and volume to her tresses than she'd ever seen.

When she was done, Trace said, "It's a Christmas miracle! What do I owe you?"

Priscilla laughed, but not quite as joyfully as before. "On the house, my friend."

"Are you sure?"

She gave Trace's hair one more gentle fluffing. "Absolutely." She bent down and whispered in her ear. "And just remember, you have a very good name."

"There you are!" Hans marched into the salon, startling them both. They swung around.

Trace noticed the subtle way Priscilla moved her body between Trace and Hans. "May I help you, Hans?" she asked.

His expression was stern, though there was something else about it Trace could not quite nail down. "The creche is missing from the chapel."

"That's terrible," Priscilla said.

He zeroed in on Trace. "What do you know about it?"

"Nothing. Have you checked with housekeeping? Or maintenance? Maybe it needed repairs."

"Or you could ask your boyfriend. He did sleep there."

Trace exchanged a glance with Priscilla, who, by the wide-eyed look on her face, appeared to be hearing that news for the first time.

"He's not my boyfriend, but I'd like to point out that, due to the ant problem—"

"That you two caused." He switched a hard hat from one hand to the other.

"Well, a whole lotta people were running through the chapel yesterday. That's all I'm saying."

"So you're defending him, then."

Was she? Whatever disappointment she felt about her mistakes where Noah was concerned, she couldn't fathom him being a thief. She thought back to the night they first met, well, after she ogled him in the lobby. Even after hours of travel, he was working, focused on getting everything just right ...

With the right tools, I could slip them right out of their frames.

She pushed that thought away. He couldn't be involved with thefts, just couldn't be. Trace slid out of the chair and looped her purse onto the crook of her arm. She turned her back to Hans. "Thank you again, Priscilla. You are very generous." Her voice cracked on the word.

"Remember what I said. Gorgeous, inside and out."

Trace nodded, but as she walked away, Hans followed her. Priscilla tried to stop him with a gentle word. "Hans, give her some space." But he ignored her and stuck close to her heels.

Trace spun around. He nearly ran into her. She put up her hand. "I'm very sorry to hear about the creche but I know nothing about it."

He opened his mouth, but before Hans could accuse her again, she said, "Don't follow me." Then she gave her head a tight shake and turned away from him.

Quickly, she walked through the building, ignoring a catcall from Thomas and a wave from other staffers. She wove through the throng of tourists milling about, shutting out the impossibly buoyant Christmas carols swirling through the crowd.

Her eyes landed on the spot where Noah had pulled her into his embrace. The memory of his cologne hit her like a gentle rain shower. She should have decked him, but instead, she'd leaned in as if a giant bushel of mistletoe had been stuck over their heads.

The tension that had ebbed away in the last hour came back with a vengeance. Noah said he had been trying to help her, and she had believed him. She thought he was being altruistic when he'd hugged her in front of Thomas, but was he trying to throw her off the track?

Had he given her a clue when he had joked about stealing windows right out of the chapel? And now the creche was gone a day after he'd slept in there?

She couldn't be that blind, could she?

His act of chivalry might have seemed as if it were lifted from the pages of a romance novel, but maybe that was all just a ... lie. When she'd first spotted Noah, she thought maybe he was an angel. That very well may have been a disguise, too.

Thomas skidded to a stop in front of her, a goofy grin on his face. "Nice hairdo. Does Santa know one of his dorky elves is missing?"

"Not now, Thomas!" The flood she'd been holding

back began to break through its flimsy barrier. She pushed past him.

"Hey, wait," Thomas called after her. "Trace?"

She ignored him. She ignored everyone while pressing through the front doors, where the familiar sound of bells gave her a modicum of comfort.

"You okay, Trace?" Hope said.

She sniffled and rooted around in her pocket for some change. She hardly ever carried cash anymore. Darn debit cards! Why had cash gone out of style?

Hope reached out and touched her elbow. "It's okay. You've given plenty."

Trace sniffled, tears flowing now.

"Oh my goodness!" Hope put down the bell and pulled Trace toward her, wrapping her in a hug. "Whatever is the matter?"

Trace began to relay some of her sadness, how her mother couldn't come for Christmas, and she hadn't spoken to her father in years, and finally, how she had fallen for a guy and he turned out not to be who she thought he was. It all came out like one giant word vomit.

Trace pulled away from Hope, sheepish from her display. "Sorry, sorry." She dabbed her eyes with a tissue Hope handed her.

"The holidays have a way of highlighting our hopelessness sometimes."

"But it's not supposed to be that way."

"Maybe not, but as I always say, the more we realize our hopelessness, the more we realize our need for a rock to lean on."

Trace swallowed. Second time in one day she'd

thought about faith's role in all of this. Had she consulted with the Lord? She twisted her mouth. Nope. She believed that Jesus was with her wherever she went, and she'd hummed along every time "What Child is This?" played over the lobby speakers.

But leaning into the faith she'd had for many years felt like a foreign concept right now, especially when her mind had put her emotions on a pedestal.

Trace wiped her tears with the back of her hand and offered Hope a shaky smile. "I'll keep that in mind," she said.

"Good. You do that. Now go home and rest. I'll be praying for you."

With little fight left in her, Trace walked to her car and let herself inside.

"Are you sure we can't talk you into flying to Maine and spending Christmas with us?" Noah's mother, Audrey, asked. He had called her to thank her for dusting off her old travel agenting skills. Thankfully, she had all of Ashley's details on file from when his ex would hire his mother to arrange her escapades.

"I'd like nothing more than to do just that," Noah said.

"You're just saying that."

He chuckled. His mother spoke her mind without a filter. She reminded him of someone he knew—or had begun to know. "Believe it or not, Mother, I am being perfectly honest."

"Then come." He could hear clicking in the background. "I'll send you a ticket."

"Stop!" He was laughing now, though it wouldn't last long. "I need to ask you something."

"Anything."

"How have you and Dad made it all these years? Relationships ... I don't know. None of them have worked out for me."

"Hold on a second." He heard shuffling in the background. "I'm putting you on speaker. Bob! Come here. Noah wants to talk to us about our love life!"

Noah scoffed, but the sound of his father's kind voice made him smile.

"What's all the commotion?"

"Hi, Dad. I was asking Mom how you two have made marriage look so cool all these years."

"That's easy. I'm a stud muffin. She says so herself."

"Oh, Bob." His mother's fake-sounding stern voice cut through.

"Well, all right then. Son, your mother makes me a better guy. I wake up every morning glad to be her husband. She may seem, how should I say this, a little aggressive—"

"I'm just assertive!"

"Right, honey, that's what I meant." His father chuckled lightly. "Truth be told, your mother is honest. And kind. And frankly, the most generous woman I've ever met. Does things on the down-low, if you know what I mean."

"On the down-low?" Noah asked.

"Yeah, you don't know the half of what she does for

people and I'm not about to tell you. That's between her and God. But as for me, I get to see it up close living in the same house." He paused, emotion rising in his voice. "It's a beautiful thing to behold."

"Aw, now you've got me crying over here," Audrey said. "You big lug."

Noah let his father's sentiments sink in. Thoughts that had already formed in his mind about Trace began to crystalize. But surely his mother, knowing Ashley for so long, would have seen right through her.

"I have something to ask you, Mother. What was it about Ashley that you thought would be so perfect for me?"

"Perfect? Oh, no-no-no. I never thought that."

He frowned. "Then why would you set us up?"

His mother unfurled one of her long and dramatic sighs. "You had such a chip on your shoulder when it came to women, Noah. You looked at your father and me as if we were stinky French cheese that you would have nothing to do with."

"That is not true. I never—"

"My son, hear me out. I knew you needed to get a woman like Ashley out of your system so I suggested you take her out. I never thought you would take it so far."

He gasped. *"That's* why you wanted me to call her so badly? To get her out of my system?"

"I was just trying to show you some contrast."

"Almost backfired, too," Bob cut in. "I told you so, Audrey. Shouldn't be messing around with a man's heart."

"True," she said. "I have never felt so much regret in my life, Noah."

"And I've never seen this woman pray so much either. She's not one to show contrition—"

"*That* is so not true, Bob!"

"It kind of is, love."

"Dad?" Noah interrupted their back-and-forth. "You were in on this?"

"I wouldn't say so, no."

Noah groaned. He ran a hand down his face, the stubble growth moving closer to the beard category.

Bob continued. "Your mother more than made up for her foible this past year. Son, I'm not gonna lie. Having you away from us has been rough."

His mother interrupted. "Very rough on your father!"

"But you're out there, finding your own way," his father continued. "I just hope you find what you're looking for, Noah."

I already have.

The thought lit up in his mind like a marquee in wintertime. He still had much to parse through, such as how his mother meddled, apparently, to teach him a lesson. One he did not readily learn, unfortunately.

But at this moment, none of that mattered. He had found what he'd been looking for, even before he knew that he was searching. The burning question in his mind now?

Could he manage to keep the real thing in his life before she slipped away from him forever?

"What's got you in a snit?" Trace frowned at Agatha, who was meowing for no apparent reason. She'd fed her, filled her water dish, and emptied the litter box. But her feline companion still had much to say.

Trace curled up on the couch and pulled a cottony throw over herself. Her phone rang, but she ignored it. It rang again, and she answered the call without bothering to look at who was calling.

"Oh good! You finally answered," Tammy said.

Her stepmother? Groan.

"Are you there, Trace?"

"Mm-hm." She sat up and pushed the blanket onto the floor. "I'm here."

"Good. You sure are a hard one to get ahold of. You work too much."

Trace rolled her eyes. She was in no mood. "Well, it is the holidays, you know."

"And that's exactly why I'm calling."

Trace perked up. She and her father hadn't been particularly close the past dozen or so years, although Tammy couldn't be blamed for that. Besides, Trace was too old to be blaming someone else for the demise of her parents' marriage. She knew this in her head, but her heart always had a hard time accepting it.

"If you're asking me to come out there, I can't this year ... work and all." Trace idly looked at her chipped fingernails.

Tammy's voice raised a pitch. "Oh, no, I wasn't going to ask that."

Oh. Did that mean they were thinking of coming out to California for once ...?

"All I wanted to know, sweetie, is what you'd like for Christmas. Your dad would like to get you something special."

Well, this was ... unexpected. She hadn't made a list in years, like she had as a kid, and so she couldn't think of a thing. Any momentary hope for something like a big family Christmas this year had splintered away. Once again, they would all spend the day clear across the country from each other, each of them opening matching gift cards on Christmas morning.

Not that she was bitter.

"So ... what's on your Santa list this year?"

Noah's face sprang to mind, but she flicked it away. She swallowed and began puttering around the living room. A thought came to mind. "Honestly, I don't need a thing—"

"But what do you want?"

Trace exhaled. "Well ... there's a women's shelter not far from here. I'd love it if you would make a donation in my name."

Tammy squealed. "Perfect! He'll love that."

Trace shrugged.

"Trace? Your dad loves you. You know that, right?"

She blinked back tears. Blast those tears again! What was up with that lately? Trace cleared her throat. "Yes, I know that. Tell him I said hello and, um, Merry Christmas."

"I will, Trace. We will talk soon, eh?"

Agatha had draped herself over the top of the couch like a melodramatic string of garland. Add a bow and Trace could wrap her around the Christmas tree and call it a day.

She sighed. Any hope for a nap for herself had gone, but it was just as well. She still had not given her notice and needed to do so soon.

But first—Christmas music. And not the same track that had been flowing through the inn's speakers. She dropped to the ground, opened the cabinet door that held her old albums, and pulled out the one wrapped in red. The color across its front was blotchy from wear, but she could still hear the songs in her mind.

"Okay, Andy," she said, "take me down memory lane now, won't you?"

With "The Christmas Song" in the background telling her to roast some chestnuts over an open fire, Trace stepped over to the table and began to re-read the contract she'd signed to begin working for The Palms. If she spent some time creating a spreadsheet with a to-do list, giving her notice to Jackson and Meg might come easier. She didn't want there to be any question about whether she could take on this new job or not.

As she listened to the music, trying to get into the magic of the season, it niggled at her that The Palms was in no condition to re-open for a while. Why, then, did Sam not say anything about that? She looked through the documents again.

Andy was wishing her a Merry Christmas for the third or fourth time when she made a sudden connection. A very bad connection.

What?

She scrutinized The Palms' logo on the top of her contract. The same logo she'd seen on the hard hat in Hans' hand earlier today. It hadn't occurred to her then, but the image had lodged itself somewhere deep in her mind.

She straightened, the realization a blow to her sternum. She had always heard that if something was too good to be true, believe it. For the past few days, she had come to understand this phrase as it applied to Noah.

But Sam too? Had he sent one of his goons to the chapel to remove the old creche? Worse ... was he stealing other items from Sea Glass Inn as well?

She'd always heard about Sam and Mr. Riley's falling out, but assumed it was all bygones now. Why hadn't she asked him about that specifically?

Trace made her way to the couch, ready to pull that old blanket over her head for the second time today. She settled for tossing it over her legs as she squeezed her eyes shut, willing away the tangle of worry.

Her eyes snapped open. Noah. She had chased away all thoughts that he could have something to do with this but now she wondered. Was he the insider making things disappear all over the place? She desperately needed this to not be true. Granted, she wasn't speaking to him, but oh! She prayed he wouldn't be a, a ... thief.

She threw off the blanket and marched across the room. Andy had moved on to "The First Noel" and she didn't want that beautiful song to be marked by this moment. Trace lifted the needle and removed the album, putting it safely away.

Agatha raised her head and watched Trace, but otherwise laid there like a boneless animal without a care. Unfortunately, she needed someone to care.

"That's it." Trace pulled on a sweater. She didn't know

exactly what she was going to do about all this, but she got into her car anyway and headed back to Sea Glass Inn.

The chapel was quiet, the altar empty-looking without the creche to hold Mary, Joseph, and Baby Jesus. Mr. Riley always insisted they not make their appearance until the day before Christmas, and it was a good thing, or they'd be gone too.

Another tree had been brought in, this one grand compared to that twig that had been eaten by ants. Still, she missed the twig (but not the ants).

Trace sighed and melted into the pew. How she had managed to slip by staff on her way in here was a miracle. She had half-expected to see a hook come out of a secret passageway and pull her over to the concierge desk, but no one had stopped her. Now all she cared to do was sit and think and pray for this mess to be revealed.

She blinked, and spotting something, moved closer to the sparsely decorated tree. Her skin flushed. Dangling from one thick branch was the drummer boy that Noah had put on the other tree, the one they had decorated together. How was it saved when nothing else was? Her heart began to thrum loudly.

She remembered how Noah had hung that ornament from a branch, saying it gave the tree meaning. Right now, for her, it did too.

Though her heart felt leaden in her chest, the innocence of that little boy and his simple drum announcing the arrival of a savior, put things into perspective. Tension rolled right out of her. There was so much more to life than the little bubble she'd found herself in, wasn't there? So what if she was never "part of the gang." She'd never really been much of a joiner anyway, so why start now?

Trace stepped back, allowing her gaze to wash over the tree, then up toward that stark cross hanging over the altar. Her heart ached, but still, she knew what she had to do.

Chapter 9

It's the Most Wonderful Time of the Year

"You seem quite serious, Trace." Jackson sat behind the mahogany desk that his father once used when he ran this inn. His hands were folded on his desk, his dark eyes questioning.

Trace wet her lips, her throat dry. Last night this had seemed so much easier in her mind. "I, yes, it is."

Meg flew into a chair next to Trace's. "I've never seen you like this. Is it your family? Are you okay?"

Jackson slid a look at his wife and then back to Trace. "We want to help you in any way we can."

Trace's throat thickened. She hadn't expected that response, especially since she hadn't told them anything yet. "Well, I might as well say it. I was planning to give my notice this week."

Meg gasped. "No! Why?"

Again, a reaction she wasn't expecting.

"I, well, I was offered what seems—seemed—like a good position, and I, uh, decided to go for it."

Meg stared wordlessly at her for a beat, then directed a concerned glance at Jackson.

"Can you tell me where you're going?" Meg asked. "Maybe there's something I can do to talk you out of it."

"That's the thing. I've decided not to take the position after all."

A smile broke out on Meg's face. "Hooray! That's good news, then!"

Jackson continued to watch Trace with a contemplative expression. "Meg, I think there's more to this story. Is there a reason you're telling us this now, Trace?"

"I think I know who has been stealing from the hotel."

Again with the exchanged glances!

She continued. "This is hard for me ... I feel, well, I feel like an idiot." Sneaky tears sprang to her eyes.

Jackson nodded. "Trace, please don't say another word. We know all about it."

She tilted her head to the side. "You ... do?"

Meg touched her arm. "Yes, unfortunately, thanks to Noah."

"*Thanks* ... to ... huh?"

"Noah told us what Sam Chambers was doing, how he figured out that he was trying to replicate the inn over at his property. I wasn't surprised. He and Dad were partners, but he has a dark side. Fought Dad every step, and when my father wouldn't agree, he'd call him soft." Jackson huffed a small laugh. "Then he pulled his funds out of the company account and left my father scrambling. He's wanted to get back at him ever since—even with him gone now."

Meg said, "The thing is, honey, none of us are exactly sure how he's getting away with it."

"Wait. So Noah told you that Sam's stealing, but he's not the one doing it?"

"He did. And from my perspective, at great sacrifice," Jackson said. "His company is bound to lose on this job, but he saw something wrong and acted on it regardless."

Meg was watching her with a thoughtful expression. "Did you think your boyfriend was stealing from the inn?"

She looked away and whispered, "He's not my boyfriend."

They exchanged a look.

Trace stood up. "Why do you keep doing that?!"

"What are we doing?" Meg said.

"You're exchanging a look!" She rolled her hand into a fist, holding it to her side. "That's what couples always do and I am sick and tired of, of … being left out."

She whipped around and headed for the door. Anti-nausea meds would come in handy right now.

"Trace, wait." Meg stopped her at the door, her expression bright. "Thank you for telling us. I hope you know how much we treasure you around here."

Trace searched Meg's face for a hint of sarcasm, but all she saw was relief. She had wanted to hear this for so long, though she hadn't realized it until recently. And now that she had, a sheepishness crept into her consciousness.

On her way out, Trace skipped the elevator and took the stairs. Chances were the lobby was so packed on these days before Christmas that no one would ever notice her. As usual.

She stepped into the fray and stopped. Deja vu hit her

like another showing of "It's a Wonderful Life" on TV. Noah was standing at the front desk, a black duffle bag at his feet. He was checking out?

Fine. She marched over and tapped a finger on his shoulder, his hard, muscular shoulder. Noah turned around. "Mornin'."

"You're checking out."

"Is that what you want?"

When she didn't answer right away, Noah flicked his chin toward the outside. "C'mon."

She walked alongside him, out the lobby doors, a million questions amassing in her mind like one of those Where's Waldo scenes. The second he turned around to face her, she said, "Where is what's-her-name?"

He didn't blink. "Gone."

"I see."

Noah towered over her, but only her heart felt threatened. "She's gone for good, Trace."

"Uh-huh." Trace ran her tongue across her teeth, thinking. She had something to say but it was getting all twisted up.

He dipped his head, peering at her, though she wasn't quite sure if she was ready to look him in the eye. "Is that what you were hoping? That I'd be checking out of here?"

She tried to center herself. He did things to her no one else could. She was Sylvester the cat, lying on the pavement with tiny birds making loop-de-loops around her head.

"Trace?"

She startled. "Sam. He, uh, told you what he was doing? That he was stealing from Sea Glass Inn?"

Noah's eyes darkened, his mouth grim. "I figured it out. Don't know all the details, but after a while, it became obvious."

Trace's shoulder sank. She exhaled.

"What?"

"I, uh, well, I figured it out too. I hoped I was wrong." She shrugged, then swallowed. "Thought maybe you had something to do with it."

He watched her for a beat, realization taking his expression from confused to horrified. "You really thought I was a criminal?"

"Well, when you put it like that it doesn't sound too good."

He scoffed. "How else should I put it then?"

Now, who was feeling guilty?

Noah's warm hand touched her cheek. He tilted her chin up with the crook of his forefinger. "I don't blame you for wondering about that. I hadn't told you I was working for Sam."

"Or that you were engaged to a beauty queen."

He cracked a smile. "We were never officially engaged. As for the beauty queen, I'm looking at one."

She swatted his hand away. In her peripheral, it appeared to her that Hope was leaning in. Trace slid a glance in her direction and widened her eyes in warning.

Hope laughed and pretended to look away.

"So what are you going to do?" Trace asked.

"I'm not sure that I know yet." He pressed his lips together, his expression rueful. "Guess I'll have to take it to my boss next and see what he wants to do about it."

"Will he, uh, be upset that you told the inn owners about your suspicion?"

"There's a very good chance of that."

"Because it could bankrupt them."

He crossed his arms and straightened his stance, peering at her. "It's the right thing to do, Trace."

"I know."

A pause fell between them. "You didn't want to speak to me the other day," he said.

"I'm aware."

"I have things to say to you. Will you hear me out?"

"What's to hear out? We were only pretending anyway, Noah. You were my hero for one shining moment and now that it's over you can go back to your regular life." She shrugged and forced a nonchalant expression onto her face. "What else is left to say?"

"The thing with Ashley is over."

"Uh-huh."

"I made that clear to her."

Trace couldn't look at him—it hurt too much and she did not like wearing her real feelings on her face. Not one bit.

"C'mon. Talk to me."

"I think you're just running away," she muttered.

"Excuse me?"

"It's obvious you and she have a lot to unpack." She licked her lips and tried her best to look him in the eyes without falling apart. "I can see why you didn't tell me about her."

"You're wrong. There's nothing left between us and no matter what you might think or how it looked, it's been that way for a long time." Noah's gaze stayed steady. "It's over, Trace."

Trace let a long pause hang there between them. Finally, she lifted her chin until their eyes met. "You told her you loved her. You said you would wait for her."

He winced. "How do you know that? Did she tell you?"

"So you admit it."

Noah groaned. "Sure I admit it, but that was before."

"You put it in writing, Noah. A girl doesn't easily forget that."

"Yeah, well, she laughed at me."

She hesitated. "What do you mean, she laughed? When you proposed or ...?"

"She laughed after reading the letter. I wrote it in earnest and she treated it like a joke." He stared at the ground now, his dark brows bunched together. "I admit that when I checked into the hotel, I was still holding a torch for her. A small one. Make that a lit match. But I realized I was just waxing poetic. I was wishing for something that could never exist."

"I see."

"Do you? I'm not so sure." He leaned in, his gaze intense. "After Ashley, I gave online dating a try. Tried to appease my parents mainly so my mother would stop trying to fix me up."

She cracked a smile.

"Oh, you laugh. But it's not funny at all. After a while, I thought, you know what? People don't fall in love anymore the way my parents did. These days you swipe left or right. I tried and failed at it all, so I swore off women.

But you're right ... I was running somewhat. When I checked into this hotel, a small part of me wondered *what if* and yearned for the marriage to Ashley that I'd hoped for."

So what happened?

"Are you kidding? *You* changed all that. You might put on this armor of toughness, but I could see your vulnerability. You are kind and generous, and whether you will admit this or not—beautiful."

"Priscilla gave my hair a makeover."

He reached out and touched her hair where it brushed across her shoulders. "Kind of her, but completely unnecessary."

She turned away. How was she to know which compliments were true and which came with a catch?

"Maybe you're the one who's running away," Noah said. "You didn't seem all that excited about starting that new job at The Palms."

"Doesn't matter anymore, though, now does it? I can't very well work for someone who is coordinating thefts from the inn. Besides, that place is miles from being done." She paused. "I wish you would have mentioned that."

"Me too, Trace. Me too." Noah's phone buzzed. He flicked a look at the screen and sighed. "I've got to take this. Talk later?"

"I suppose."

He gave her a smile that told her he wouldn't be taking no for an answer.

After Noah left, Hope approached her. "You sure are giving that young man a hard time."

Trace shrank back, feeling every bit as incredulous as she must have looked.

She clucked her tongue. "I know a fake standoff when I see one."

"Is that so?"

"You like him. And it's a good thing, too, since he's obviously not the one causing havoc around here."

"Hmm. Yeah."

Hope wrinkled her brow. "What is it?"

"If Noah's not the one doing all the stealing for Sam, who is?"

Trace woke to a streak of sun filtering through her window sheers. The wind had howled all night long. Outside on the street below, drifts of brown leaves were scattered about. Jan's fat plastic snowman had fallen over too, and a crow was sitting on top of it, pecking at its black top hat as if the accessory was a personal footstool.

Meow.

She cast a long look at Agatha who had, apparently, spotted the wayward crow, too. "Now, now," she said, giving her cat several soft strokes, "it's Christmastime. Try not to want to eat that bird, okay?"

Meow.

In the kitchen, Trace brewed a pot of coffee and took a deep breath while the water made its way through the ground-up beans. She poured a cup and waited a few minutes longer until she had a chance to consume several large sips of caffeine before calling Sam.

"Well if it isn't Miss Murphy."

"Hello, Sam."

"What can I do for you this bright morning?"

She had already determined not to mention the missing items from Sea Glass Inn, though it might have helped her break her news to him. But Jackson said they were still trying to determine how Sam was getting away with the thievery, and she did not want to get into the middle of that.

This didn't mean she wouldn't dig a little herself.

"I'm sitting here having a cup of coffee and enjoying the sunny morning as well, Sam. And I was thinking of my visit to the property recently."

"I hope you were pleased."

"Mm. Well, it was hard to see all the changes, all that plastic everywhere."

"Will be gone before you know it!"

"Right. Yes. But now that I've had a few days to reflect, I couldn't but help notice the similarities everywhere to Sea Glass Inn."

"Oh?"

"You don't see them?"

"Well, I—" He stopped talking and she heard paper shuffling. "They say that imitation is the highest form of flattery, don't they?"

What about stealing?

Naturally, she didn't say that out loud. "You're right. I've heard that many times. That's why knock-offs sell so well at discount stores."

"Yes. So. What else can I do for you today?"

"So you admit that The Palms' renovations are being modeled after Sea Glass Inn?"

"Never said that. Why would I want such a thing?"

She paused, noting the change in the tone of Sam's voice. "You told me at lunch that you and Mr. Riley were great friends, and I'm wondering about that. Can you tell me a little bit about the falling out that has been rumored?"

Sam cleared his throat, the manner gruff. "Is that what this is all about?"

"I thought it would be appropriate for me to know some of your history. Something I could share with the guests, and potential conference bookings. You know, a sort of peek into the past. He was quite well-known around here, after all."

"There will be none of that with our guests. Understood?"

"Why ever not?" She waited. "Unless there's a reason you don't want anyone to know about your past friendship with Mr. Riley ...?"

"That old man was not my friend. Everything he created was my idea." His tone had dropped further, the sound foreboding. The image of Sam as a kindly old man rebuilding an old property into a delightfully appointed boutique hotel faded away. "Bottom line is old Riley stole from me and I don't care to hear that man's name anywhere in my hotel. Am I understood?"

"I don't think I can agree to that, sir. Mr. Riley will always have a very special place in my heart, God rest his soul."

Silence.

Sam spoke first. "Then I don't think you are the right fit for this hotel, Ms. Murphy. And since your employment here has not officially started, it would be best if we cancel your contract." He paused. "You'll be able to save face that way."

Relief rushed through her like the ripple of a warm, salty wave dissipating onto the shore. "On the contrary, sir. My reputation will hold up either way. But I will take you up on your offer to cancel the contract. It's for the best."

"Yes, it is." He hung up without a goodbye.

Hours later, Trace entered Sea Glass Inn with mixed feelings. Her heart felt lighter, but an under-the-surface niggling still poked at her when she stepped behind the concierge desk for the thousandth or so time. Maybe it was the fact that she'd just ended a dream contract before it started, or it might have been that she even had to. Or maybe it was something altogether different that bothered her, though she couldn't figure out what.

"Excuse me?" A middle-aged woman with rosy cheeks and a pretty updo stood at the counter. "Could you help me choose a restaurant for dinner tonight?"

"That would be my pleasure. How many?"

"Three. I hope." Silence fell, and she added, "My kids are supposed to come tonight, but they don't always make it."

Trace smiled kindly. "Let's plan on all three of you." She reviewed several options, depending on the type of food the woman thought her family would prefer. When the woman picked The Windsor Knot, Trace said, "Good choice. I have an idea. Let's have the restaurant text your children with the details of your reservation."

The woman's face lit up. "Will it include the menu?"

"Yes, ma'am."

"That's a wonderful idea!"

Once she'd gone, Trace allowed herself to breathe in the holiday spirit weaving through the lobby. Stephanie worked on the lobby marquee, adding directions to the chapel for Christmas morning. The cafe staff buzzed around in a tizzy adding new black tablecloths throughout —an upgrade that would last through New Year's Eve, and other staffers were setting up the ballroom for a huge Christmas Eve shindig being put on by an insurance company. Not the way she would want to spend Christmas Eve, but maybe they were handing out bonuses or something.

She exhaled. Bing Crosby's "White Christmas" played over the speakers, and though there was no snow to be found, Christmas truly was in full swing at the inn.

Thomas appeared in front of her, a goofy grin on his face. "Hey there—"

She faced him head-on. "Why don't you like me, Thomas?"

His grin dropped like the log ride at Knott's Berry Farm. "Who says I don't like you?"

"Well," she said, crossing her arms and leveling a look at him, "you say mean things to me all the time."

For the first time in the years that she had known and worked with Thomas, he didn't have a retort. Nothing to sling back at her. Just a slack-jawed, deer-in-the-headlights expression dragging down his cheekbones. "I, uh, dunno."

"What kind of answer is that?"

"A terrible one?"

She nodded.

The color came back to his face, and he firmed up his stance. Thomas leaned one hand on the counter, stole a look over his shoulder, then swung his chin back in her direction. "Maybe it means I like you."

She scrunched her nose. "Like we're in junior high or something?"

He shrugged. "I guess."

"Well, it hurts my feelings." Phew. Getting that off her chest was ... freeing, but Thomas's expression crashed worse than before.

"I'm sorry, Trace. I always thought it was, you know, our thing. Our bit."

"Bit?"

"Like we were flirting."

"Wait. You really do like me?"

He clamped a hand at his waist. "You've been flirting with me for, like, a hundred years. I'm sorry that I hurt your feelings. I never meant to do that."

By the contrition in his expression, Trace knew he was being honest—and it floored her. She saw him in a completely different way now. Truth was, she was most comfortable shooting off her mouth first and thinking about it later. Had she been an unwitting accomplice in his teasing?

Maybe.

"For what it's worth," she said, "I wouldn't know how to flirt if Ryan Gosling knocked on my door with a bouquet of daisies and a diamond necklace."

Thomas snorted a laugh. "You would too."

She shifted. "For heaven's sake, if you thought I was

flirting with you, why didn't you just say something rather than call me names?"

He swallowed, looking as if he were searching for the right words. He took another glance over his shoulder. Noah was leaning against a pillar in the distance, talking on his cell phone. When Thomas swung his glance back to her, he said, "I keep asking myself that very same thing."

She raised her brows as he slapped the counter, pointed a finger gun at her, and said, "Good talk."

Then she watched him jog away.

Chapter 10

I'll Be Home for Christmas (redux)

"**W**ill you still spend the eve of your birth with me?" Noah asked.

She hadn't seen very much of Noah the past couple of days. From what she'd heard, his job was in question. He strode through the lobby on several occasions, AirPods in his ears, eyes straight ahead, mouth moving, hands flexing.

There was also the awkwardness of their relationship. Well, their fake relationship that had turned real, only no one knew it had been fake in the first place.

See? Awkward.

"You're asking me to spend Christmas Eve with you?"

"Thought we could go to a nice dinner. Get reacquainted. I'll wear something other than denim."

"You'd better not."

He laughed, his grin wide. "Whoa, there. Control yourself, young lady."

"I suppose I could commit to dinner out with you. It is my birthday eve, after all."

"I'll take that as a yes. Pick you up at seven."

Fortunately, Trace managed to have that day off. One perk of being on staff for as many years as she'd been was knowing when the vacation calendar would be released online—and she had been ready. Of course, another "perk" of being around so long was being cornered by her boss to work on Christmas Day, aka her birthday.

Her heart sank ever so slightly at the thought of Christmas this year. For one, it hurt to hear her mother sound so uninterested in seeing her, as if work took precedence over their relationship. In some ways, that was a cautionary tale she was determined to heed for the future.

She also thought this would be the last Christmas that she spent at Sea Glass Inn. It wasn't staying at the inn that she was sad about, really, but the loss of the dream to finally be recognized for her contributions. Maybe Priscilla was right. She needed to see herself the way God did and ask for what she wanted.

She stood in front of the mirror, examining the form-fitting dress she'd chosen for the night, a brighter color than she usually wore. She'd bought it right off the rack at one of the cute little boutiques downtown. Even paid full price. For some reason, she was feeling ... risky.

The doorbell rang. Trace stood in the quiet a moment, well, quiet except for a single meow of protest from Agatha. "Hush, you."

Noah barreled into her life less than a month ago, but it didn't feel that way. It felt more like he had picked her up at the bottom of a giant rollercoaster, pulled her inside the car with him, and together they'd climbed and dipped and jostled their way through one adventurous December.

She let those heady thoughts sink in. Maybe this wouldn't be forever (she hoped it might be), but for now, she decided to heed Priscilla's advice and let herself feel the moments as they presented themselves.

The doorbell rang again. "What do you think, Agatha? Does this dress make me look fat?"

Meow.

"I'm gonna take that as a no," Trace said over her shoulder as she padded to the front door after the bell rang.

She flung the door open to find Noah standing there, his gaze both new and familiar and ... tantalizing. His eyes trailed up her body. Instead of shrinking back, Trace struck a pose.

"Gorgeous," he said, his voice husky.

"What can I say? It's the new me."

Noah stepped inside. He handed her a breathtaking bouquet of wildflowers. She made a mental tick mark for another phenomenon that she was experiencing for the first time: Hot man bringing flowers—check.

"I'll put these in water." She wandered over to the kitchen to fetch a vase, but not before sending Agatha a *Don't be a brat* glare. By the time she turned around again, Agatha had dropped onto the ground and was investigating Noah's pant leg.

"She likes you," Trace said while reaching into a drawer under her kitchen island. "Here." She handed him a lint roller.

He looked from the roller to the cat and back to Trace. "Ah. White cat, black slacks."

"'Ah' is right."

He made quick work of his pant leg as Trace gently shooed Agatha back toward the couch.

"I'm guessing I shouldn't sit there."

"Not unless you want to roll that over your bum."

He chuckled. "I'll pass. Ready to go?"

A flicker of disappointment passed through Trace when they pulled up in front of Sea Glass Inn. Did he forget his wallet? His cellphone? Those questions were answered when he stepped out of his truck and came around to open her door for her.

"Watch your step," he said, holding his arm out for support. In his other hand, he held a bottle of red wine. When he caught her eyeing it, he said, "I've been holding onto it for a special occasion."

As they strolled wordlessly into the hotel lobby, she missed the trill of the bells. Hope would have gone home by now, but she missed hearing the sound regardless.

"Good evening," one of the newer bellmen, Duke, greeted them.

They murmured their greetings in response. By the time they entered the lobby, whirling with finely dressed guests, the air heavy with festive carols, Trace had resigned herself. Quite obviously, they would be spending the evening in the cafe. At least the tablecloths were new. And he'd brought his own wine.

"Have I told you how beautiful you look tonight?" Noah whispered.

She slid a glance to the man whose hand was squarely wrapped around hers. Mm-hm, she wasn't imagining this. "You might have mentioned it."

"It's still true."

She smiled, all hint of disappointment dissipating. They reached the hall near the bank of elevators, the cafe's doors in sight. With the dimmed lighting and the twinkling of white lights throughout, it looked like a dreamland.

"Noah? Hey, Noah, is that you?" Jackson was jogging down the hall toward them, concern lacing his voice. He landed a hand on Noah's shoulder. "Hey, man, you're just the guy I need to see."

Trace's gaze went from Noah's to Jackson's and back again.

"What can I help you with?" Noah asked.

She nearly let out a yelp of protest, but bit it back. Jackson was an awful lot like his father, who ruled this roost before him. He didn't back down from a project easily, and if Noah didn't outright refuse, she feared she'd spend her birthday watching him bent beneath a counter with his sleeves rolled up.

Noah turned to her. "This'll only take a minute and we've got time before our reservation. Come with me?"

She shrugged and put on the concierge smile she'd been wearing for a decade. "Sure. Of course."

You know that disappointment that flickered earlier before disappearing? The way Jackson was explaining how he needed Noah's help with a broken window, and Noah's eagerness to please, that flicker had turned into an all-out power outage.

"I didn't even know you knew Jackson that well," Trace whispered as they hurried along down the hall.

Noah shrugged, his smile good-natured. "He's seen me

around, and then when I told him about Sam's plan, we ended up talking all things construction."

"Hm. I see."

Jackson turned the corner. "It's right in here." He pulled open one of the oversized ballroom doors. It was dark inside.

"We're gonna need some light," Noah said.

With a whoosh, the ballroom lights switched on and an entire room full of people yelled, "SURPRISE!"

This moment could best be described as ... unexpected. Like the time you find the cherished possession that you thought was long lost. And there it is, sitting among the dust bunnies behind your overflowing hamper.

She never expected this—to see so many she knew and cared for in one place, crushing around her as if she were some sort of celebrity. The air crackled with surprise, pure and untarnished. A banner hung on one wall: *Happy (Milestone) Birthday, Trace!*

Tears pressed against her eyes, but she didn't fight them. Noah grasped her hand tighter and she twisted a look toward him.

"Did you know?"

He grinned. "I was given an inkling."

She grinned back. "Inkling. That's a good word."

He leaned toward her, his voice a growl. "They all love you."

Liddy butted in. "Happy Birthday, my friend! Oh, I love you so much!" She smacked a kiss on her cheek.

Her husband, Beau, bent down and gave her a hug. "Many happy returns, beautiful."

Meg, too, pulled her into a hug, rocking her back and forth like a mama bear. "We got you, didn't we?"

"I-I'm still trying to figure out wh-what's going on."

"Ha—we did, then! And by the way, you're not working on Christmas Day! That was only to make sure you didn't go out of town or something."

Trace laughed. *As if.* She looked around at the crowd, one unending grin. From the corner of her eye she saw Jackson give Noah a bro hug. Would wonders never cease ...?

Hope approached her, smiling. Her friendly bellringer friend gave Trace a warm hug and a small pot planted with pansies. "Happy Birthday and Merry Christmas all rolled into one!"

"Thank you!" Trace said. "I'm so happy that you're here."

"Me too." She swallowed, surveying the room. "You inspire so many."

Though Hope was being serious, Trace didn't know how to take that. She still wondered if this was all some sort of mirage. She followed Hope's gaze to the servers taking their place along one wall where tables were filled with food from end to end. Sure looked—and smelled—real, though.

Meg slid an arm around Trace's neck and turned her toward the rest of the partygoers. "Fun night ahead, girl-friend, but first, more surprises."

Trace blinked. "Is that ... Daddy?"

A man with a white goatee and round spectacles à la

Santa Claus approached, a slight blonde next to him. He gave her a tentative smile. "Happy Birthday, Punkin."

She slid a look to Tammy who gently pushed her father toward her. "But you called for my wish list."

Tammy turned her palms over and shrugged. "Your friends put me up to it. They nearly threatened with bodily harm if I gave away the secret."

Meg laughed, then swung a harsh look on her. "Good thing you complied."

They all laughed again. Her father pulled her into a hug so warm and wonderful she thought she might pass out from the shock of seeing him after so much time.

"I can't believe you came all this way," Trace said.

Her father's eyes clouded. "Anything for you, my daughter. I am so happy you'd have me."

Losing it right there in front of everybody was a very real possibility.

"Trace?" She turned. Beautiful Sophia, the inn's fashionable silent partner, took Trace's hands in hers and kissed her on both cheeks. "You are stunning. This dress suits you."

She warmed from the top of her head to the very smallest of toes. Having someone like Sophia offer her this compliment was a gift in itself. Had Sophia really chosen to spend her Christmas Eve here?

Trace gasped, then. CJ Capra was in the house! Her favorite author, even if he didn't write mysteries. The man could wield a pen in the fantasy realm and, oh, she loved the way he worked in a romance too. Sophia, his wife, had something to do with that, no doubt.

"Trace!"

"My favorite author, in the flesh! I'm honored you came out of your writing cave for me."

CJ could be a hermit when he wrote, a known fact, but he also had a humorous spirit that came out after the writing was done. His face reddened lately, that scar of his turning dark. He flashed a smile at her and she thought her knees might buckle right there. "I would not have missed this for anything, Trace, the beloved."

"Trace, the beloved. Like a character in one of your novels!" She held a hand to her heart. "Now I can die and go to heaven."

Sophia beamed at her husband.

Another familiar voice came through the crowd. "There will be no dyin' on my watch!"

Trace whirled around. "Mother!"

"It's me. All the way from Florida to wish the best daughter ever a happy birthday."

Trace's expression fell. "You're ... you're in a wheelchair." A woman who Trace didn't recognize leaned on the wheelchair's handles.

"This is Natty, my nurse."

"Short for Natasha," the woman said. "Happy birthday!"

Trace bent low and leaned her hand on the chair's armrest. "Mom?" She searched her mother's dark eyes, noting a droop to them she had never seen before. Usually, those eyes were vigilant, and unblinking—two qualities she'd honed in her own work. "Why are you in a wheelchair? Is it ... is it the MS?"

Her mother blinked, and her eyes cleared to a certain

toughness. "Yeah, it's starting to take over but it hasn't taken me out!"

Trace shook her head slowly. "I don't understand. Why didn't you tell me? I-I should have known about this sooner."

Her mother leveled a pointed look at her. "Because you would have dropped everything to come out and take care of me. I won't have any of that!" She looked over her shoulder. "Isn't that right, Natty?"

The nurse nodded. "Yup, she said that."

"That's what I've got her for anyway." She wagged a thumb at Natty.

A tear dripped from Trace's eye, but Dinah grabbed her by the hand. "I didn't come all the way out here to see you cryin' on your birthday, you hear me?"

Trace nodded.

"Good. If you need to know, I'm not in this contraption all day. Just when I'm tired, which I am because of the travel. I'm still working and analyzing evidence six days a week. Now." She snapped a look upward. "Who's that tall drink of water mooning over you?"

Noah took that opportunity to step forward and reach out to take her mother's hand. "Noah Bridges. It's a pleasure to meet you."

She shook his hand firmly and winked at Trace. "I like him."

Noah helped Trace up. He gently rubbed her back, letting her know he understood.

Another familiar voice grabbed her attention. "Hello everyone, and welcome to Trace Murphy's Christmas Eve Birthday Bash!" Thomas was manning the DJ setup at the front of the room. "Let's get this party started with a little bit of Mariah, shall we?"

Trace smiled at the unbelievability of it all, yet still in shock over her mother's condition. As partygoers began moving to the dance floor, she stole another look at her mother. Dinah waved her out there with a sweep of her hands and one stern motherly look that said *Have a fabulous time—or else!*

Next thing she knew, those iconic bells played out and Noah was pulling her into his arms. "I never knew you could dance to Christmas music," she said. "It's like the Christmas wish I never knew I had."

He molded her to him, a sweet smile on his face. "Well, then, let me make your wish come true."

Noah whirled her around the dance floor, with others joining in, as Mariah sang out, "*All I want for Christmas is you (baby).*" He broke away from her and started snapping his fingers and making faces and dancing like a fool. Then he began pretending to pull her toward him like a mime with an invisible rope.

Trace hadn't laughed this hard in she-didn't-know-when. Not the real kind of laughter, anyway, the kind that bubbled from the belly and wrapped itself around a person's windpipe like a cluster of happy elves.

When the music transitioned to something softer, Priscilla appeared at her side, her daughter, Amber, not far behind. Trace fanned herself with her hand, and automatically, Priscilla began primping Trace's hair.

"Mom!" Amber scolded. The young teen then gave Trace a conspiratorial nod. "I feel your pain. She's *always* doing that to me too."

Priscilla's husband, Wade, shook his head, chuckling. "She can't help herself."

Trace smiled. "Did you have anything to do with all of this, Priscilla?"

"We all did, darling." Priscilla waved her arm graciously, similar to a ballerina, and like magic, Sophia, Meg, and Liddy appeared and huddled around her.

"*All* of you did?"

Noah wrapped his arms around Trace from behind. "The four of them pushed me into a corner after my breakfast. Priscilla was carrying her shears and I thought she was going to use them on my head if I didn't comply."

Priscilla nodded. "There was a real possibility of that, darling."

Giggles punctuated the air around them.

"We had this whole thing pretty much under wraps until Liddy nearly outed us," Meg said.

"That's right," Priscilla said with a clap and a finger pointed toward Liddy.

Liddy shrank back. "Moi?"

Meg rolled her eyes. "You and your selfies on social media!"

"Mm-hm, that's right," Sophia murmured. "I'd forgotten because I hadn't seen the photo for myself." Sophia'd had her own troubles with social media, which had pushed her to abandon it for herself and hire an assistant to manage all that for her fashion brand.

Meg tipped her head toward Trace. "We were planning your party that night at dinner. So worried you'd see the photo and start asking questions."

For the second time tonight, Trace blinked, stunned by

revelations. That photo had been seared into her mind since the moment she'd happened upon it, and though she'd tried to label it as *no big deal,* and tuck away the memory, it had shaped her thoughts over the past few weeks.

Heat reached her face and she broke eye contact with everyone. As she stared at the carpet, her thoughts hovered there, caught between the lies she believed and the reality she had walked into tonight. If she lifted her head right now, would they all still be staring back at her with love in their eyes?

Or had she dreamed this entire night?

"Group hug!" Meg said, probably sensing Trace's wobbly emotions. She was good about that.

All four women, plus Amber, encircled her with a hug and lots of laughter. When they pulled away, she noted the serious expression on Meg's face. "Unfortunately, I do have one bit of news that I should probably spill right now."

"Yeah, get it over with," Liddy said.

Trace tilted her head to the side. "News?"

Meg sighed and exchanged a glance with Jackson, who hovered nearby. Meg splayed her hands in front of her. "Sorry! I know you don't like those glances."

Trace coughed a laugh. "Oh my gosh ... I'm an idiot. Forget about that!"

"No, you're not," Meg said. One by one each of the women, her friends, echoed that sentiment.

Jackson cut in. "Let this news come from me. It's Hans. He's been fired."

"Fired?"

"Yeah. He was Sam's inside guy, unfortunately."

Trace's mouth popped open and she exchanged an equally surprised glance with Noah. She abruptly stopped. "Oops."

Meg cracked up. "You two are already giving each other *the look*."

"That's super cute!" Liddy said, to which Trace rolled her eyes. "Yeah, yeah, I know you think Beau and I were—"

"Are."

Liddy laughed. "That we *are* gross. But, hey"—she wagged her eyes at Noah—"don't knock it, am I right?"

"Anyway," Meg said, interrupting them. "We just wanted to clear up the last piece of the Sam puzzle before a lot of rumors started."

"I'm so shocked. Oh my goodness! How did you figure it out?"

"Hope told us." Sophia turned, smiling until Hope approached the group.

"I'm afraid it's true," Hope said. "I saw Hans taking the creche. He didn't see me for some reason. I didn't think anything strange about it at the time, but then I overheard one of the valets mentioning that things were missing." She shrugged. "I'd seen Hans taking a lot of those things out of the hotel, so I put two and two together."

"Wow. You're a regular sleuth. That's amazing ... and so sad."

"I'll say." Meg twisted up her mouth. "He'd been with us for as long as you, but I guess he was disgruntled."

"He was trying to replicate Sea Glass over at Sam's hotel, then he was planning to run the whole place. Probably still is."

Sophia gave her brother a nudge before saying, "Enough of this. We are here to celebrate Trace tonight. We have food and drink and—"

"Dancing!" Christian grabbed Trace's hand and pulled her out onto the dance floor. She was living a dream and didn't want to wake up. Sophia had always said that CJ hooked her with his humor, and by the silly faces he was making, and the equally strange dance moves, she understood.

When she thought she'd pass out from laughing so hard, Noah showed up. "May I cut in?"

CJ bowed like a prince straight out of a holiday romcom, then jogged over and pulled his very proper wife onto the dance floor. Noah hugged her close, both of them laughing at CJ's antics with Sophia as they danced by.

So much to take in—longtime inn staffers from every department, the decor and music, and her parents were here! Both of them, though her mother ... she swallowed back her thoughts about the wheelchair because she'd promised to celebrate tonight. Someday, maybe tomorrow, Trace would sit in the quiet of her lighted Christmas tree, with Agatha purring on her lap, and reflect on all of this, but for now, her mind whirled and dipped, much like Noah and her on this dance floor.

"Boy, does everyone adore you around here."

"I always figured they thought I was weird."

"Maybe they love your weirdness."

She fake gasped. He laughed and tipped his head forward until their noses touched. He closed his eyes, and the intimacy of it made her knees weak. They were swaying now and she ran her gaze down his face, his neck.

His Adam's apple shifted, as if he were about to speak and she snapped a look back up.

"I'm falling for you hard, Miss Murphy."

A smile found her mouth. "You make me sound like a schoolmarm. Or a librarian."

"Kinda fits. I've been learning from you from the day we met."

"Oh, yeah?"

"Yeah. I've never met anyone so smart and funny and generous." His eyes were open now and he was looking right into hers. "All those things wrapped into a most beautiful woman."

"Beautiful, huh?"

He grinned, the huskiness of his voice taking her to a deep place. "Happy Birthday, gorgeous." His hands cupped her waist, and his face tipped over hers as he captured her gaze with his. Then Noah Bridges kissed Trace Murphy right there in front of everyone. Only this time it was real—and he wasn't doing it for show.

When Trace opened her eyes again, her father was standing next to them, one white eyebrow lifted above the rim of his glasses. "I don't suppose your old man could get a dance with his daughter." She was thirty-six years old, or would be tomorrow, yet her father eyed her date like he'd just showed up to take her to the back-to-school dance wearing leather pants.

Some women might be irked by that, but Trace was captivated.

Noah winked at her and backed away, ushering her father forward with a sweep of his arm. In a blink, Trace fast-forwarded to what, someday, might be.

As her father waltzed her around the room, Trace's mind replayed the past hurts. They would have to, one day, talk it out and forgive each other for missed events and holidays. But for now, they danced and smiled and maybe, just maybe, began the process of healing in their father-daughter relationship.

"Is that your stomach growling?" her father asked.

She giggled. "You have good hearing ..."

That white eyebrow jumped up again. "For an old man?"

She laughed outright now. "I'm starved!"

"Well, then"—he offered her the crook of his arm—"let's eat."

On their way to the lavish table of freshly made food, they passed Dinah and Hope who seemed to have struck up a friendship. Her mother was showing both Hope and Natty something on her phone, then they all reared back in laughter.

"I put some baby pictures on here!" Dinah shouted, holding up her phone.

Trace shook her head, a stupid grin finding her.

The rest of the night spun by with unfettered cheer and alarming amounts of food consumed, and though she didn't want it to end, midnight was nearly upon them. Instead of worrying that it would all fall away and her chariot would turn back into a pumpkin, Trace sensed that this night would carry her through both peaks and valleys in the future.

As if hearing her thoughts, Thomas lowered the ballroom lights, leaving nothing to guide them all but the white, lit-up strings encircling the walls and Christmas trees. Oh, and a huge cake with thirty-six candles blazing on top.

"Gather around, everyone," Thomas said. "It's time to say goodbye to Trace's mid-thirties!"

Laughter ensued.

"Ha ha ha, Thomas," Trace said.

Liddy, whom Thomas once dated, said, "You should talk, old man!"

More laughter until the first notes of "Happy Birthday" began to play. As the clock struck midnight, the entire room broke out in song, all eyes on Trace. When they reached the part, "Happy Birthday, dear Trace," more than one person added "and Jesus!" The sound of the Lord's name washing over her on the most exhilarating night of her life brought a lump to her throat. As if to put an exclamation mark on an already extraordinary night, for his last play of the night, Thomas chose "Oh Holy Night."

On their way out of the ballroom, as guests were talking and laughing and taking selfies, Noah grabbed her by the hand and pulled her around the corner, out of view.

"What are—"

He didn't wait, and kissed her there again, in the quiet nook. Her entire body tingled, and for some reason, a visual of her heart expanding popped into her mind, like that old grinch's did in the cartoon classic.

Noah smiled at her, still cradling her face in his hands. "The happiest of birthdays to you, Trace."

Her breath caught at the tenderness in his voice, and

the tears came. She hadn't experienced so many tears in years, and certainly not this kind—the happy ones. She was embarking on new things ahead. Trace felt sure of it.

Her parents had booked rooms in the hotel, so with a promise to meet them in the chapel on Christmas morning, she and Noah left. They walked hand-in-hand through the lobby doors and into the parking lot. As they reached Noah's truck, something flashed in the corner of Trace's eye. She squinted in the night.

"What is it?" Noah asked.

"I'm not exactly sure." She gestured for him to follow her. When she reached the sedan that had caught her eyes two rows back, Hope was leaning against the driver's side door. "Hope?" she asked. "Are you okay?"

Hope's eyes shimmered, and the circles under her eyes deepened. "I-I lost my keys."

"Oh!" Trace said. "And you look so tired. Let us help you."

"When was the last time you remembered having them on you?" Noah asked.

"I think it was this morning. I locked the car and went to my station at the front doors."

Noah nodded. "But you went home before the party, right?"

"I, uh ..."

Trace's eyes had become fixated on the contents of Hope's car, illuminated by their phones lit up to search for keys. Blankets, pillows, clothing. She frowned. "I don't want to pry, but Hope ... are you sleeping in your car?"

For a second, Hope's expression steeled, like she was going to deny it. But then, she slumped against the car, lowering her chin. "It's temporary until I can get back on my feet."

A catch formed in Trace's throat. "How ... how long have you been without a home?"

She let out a weary sigh. "A long time."

"Oh, Hope." She began to rub the woman's arm. "I'm so sorry. I honestly had no idea."

"I usually come early and stay late, but I always drive somewhere else to sleep." She lifted her chin. "That's how come I figured out what Hans was doing."

Noah and Trace exchanged a glance. "You saw him from the car," Trace said, a whoosh of a sigh coming from her. "No wonder he was careless."

Noah began walking around the car and trying the doors. "Wow," he said. "Hans didn't know he was being watched."

"Wow is right," Trace said.

Hope yawned. "Your party was so much fun. Thank you for inviting me."

Trace bit her lip.

"Well, I mean, thank you for being my friend so Meg thought to invite me. It was magical. Really, really."

Trace nodded. "Oh, I so agree. But ... you can't stay this way."

The creak of a hinge drew their attention. Noah was standing next to the passenger side of the car, the door fully open. He held up his hand, keys dangling from his fingers. "Found them."

Hope noticeably perked up. "I'm so thankful, Noah! So sorry to have bothered you on your big night. I will forever be grateful." She pulled open the driver's side door.

"Not so fast," Trace said. "You will not be sleeping here tonight, Hope."

Hope frowned and sneaked a glance toward the inn. "No, of course not. I will drive—"

Trace shook her head and pulled her into a bear hug, hugging her tightly. When she stepped back, her eyes filled. "You're coming home with me." Those pesky tears streamed down her cheek now.

"Oh, no." Hope shook her head. "I couldn't."

Trace would not be deterred. She held onto her new friend. "Oh, yes, you can." She swallowed back the tears. "Everyone deserves to wake up at home on Christmas morning."

Epilogue

O ne Year Later

"I can't believe a year has already gone by." Trace tossed tinsel onto the massive Christmas tree that maintenance had managed to fit through the chapel doors.

Noah winked. "One amazing year."

Trace thought about that. It truly had been magical in many ways. But she had also experienced things she'd rather not relive, like confronting Hans at the grocery store one crisp spring day.

"Why'd you do it?" she had asked him.

He was wearing his usual uniform of a shirt and tie, but the part in his hair looked jagged and he was in need of a good trim around the ears. "To get to where I am."

"Which is?" Trace held him with one sharp glance. By the sound of reviews, The Palms was still in a state of disrepair and guests weren't being kind about it.

"I'm the general manager of an up-and-coming resort. Would never have gotten there with Riley in the way."

As a gesture of goodwill, Riley Holdings didn't press charges as long as the items were returned. But the company Noah worked for pulled out of the project, not wanting to face liability for the owner's actions. Word was the hotel had been scrambling to find a replacement contractor ever since but had been limping by with help from local handymen.

"So you felt it was okay to climb the ladder by any means."

"I did what I had to do."

She could have accepted that and pushed her grocery cart down the aisle, but she had more to say. "That's the difference between you and me."

"What's that?"

"People matter. So does honor. And what you did, sir, was dishonorable."

He did that little chin jerk thing then, a sour grin on his face. Even now her stomach sank a little remembering it. Before turning away from her, Hans said, "Yeah, well, enjoy being a concierge for the rest of your life."

She watched him walk away, his shirt untucked in the back. Sure, she could have told him she had been promoted, but he would find out soon enough. The thought of gloating did not appeal to her.

"Quarter for your thoughts?" Noah asked, bringing her

to the present. She gave him a funny little smile and he shrugged. "Inflation and all."

She laughed lightly and stepped back to assess the tree. Lights and ornaments clung to its branches, but it was missing something. She tossed more tinsel on those branches, hoping that icing would do the trick. "I can't get over the developments from last year. Who knew!"

"Crazy."

"I mean, first Hope comes to live with me and Agatha takes to her like catnip. Then Mom moves to California after telling me she was an East coaster forever." She shook her head.

"And now, Hope has taken over for Natty as your mom's caregiver." Noah's voice turned husky. "God certainly knew what he was doing when he set all that in motion."

"Oh, yes, He did. Already those two are solving crimes together, with Hope assisting Mom at every turn." She added a snowman ornament to the tree, reflecting on the past year. "Faith is confidence in what we hope for."

"And assurance about what we do not see," Noah said.

Oh, *this* man. The gratitude that had begun to grow in her last year had doubled in size since then. She wondered if she could manage to contain it all.

Noah sidled up behind Trace as she tried to reach an upper branch with a star ornament and wrapped his arms around her middle. She laughed now and tried to slap away his hands. "You're going to get me fired."

"Not a chance." He whirled her around and nuzzled her neck.

She shrieked and pulled away.

Trace had chosen a holiday playlist to stream through her phone, and Eartha Kitt had begun to purr her way through "Santa Baby." Noah pulled her toward him again and hummed a line or two in her ear.

"You're ridiculous." She giggled, pushing him back again.

"What can I say? I'm a guy in love."

Goose bumps raised on her arm. He lifted his brows and she tossed some tinsel on his head.

Noah gasped and tackled her into a pew, one that thankfully had a Christmas blanket thrown across it to cushion the landing. She could barely hear someone's throat clearing over her laughter.

"Where would you like me to put these boxes, Boss?" Hannah, her head concierge, was trying to keep a straight face.

Trace extricated herself from Noah's grasp. She stood and smoothed the wrinkles out of her blouse. *Dignity, people!* "Over there would be great." She pointed to the steps leading to the altar on the other side of the tree. This year, the complete manger scene, Jesus and all, was intact up on that altar.

"Hannah?"

Hannah seemed to be struggling to make eye contact. "Mm-hm?"

"Let's keep this to ourselves, okay?"

She nodded, but a snort came out.

Trace cocked a hip. "What?"

Hannah shook her head. "Nothing, except you two"— she pointed from Noah to Trace and back again—"aren't exactly a well-kept secret."

Noah looped his arm around Trace's neck. "And I aim to keep it that way."

Trace wagged her head, sliding a look at him. There was a skip in her voice. "What's gotten into you?"

She expected him to shrug and make a joke. Instead, he seemed to pause, soberness coming over him. Chills danced up her arm for the second time today and Trace gave him a questioning smile.

Hannah laughed outright. "You two crack me up." She turned to leave. "If you need anything, I'll be at the desk all evening. But somehow, I think you'll both be fine."

Trace pouted at Noah. "You scared my employee."

He coughed a laugh. "Me? You're the big boss, so you probably leave them shaking in their boots."

"Oh, brother. Yes, that's me. Totally scary." After Hans's quick exit from Sea Glass Inn last year, Jackson wasted no time in offering Trace the position of Operations Manager. She had been revamping and reorganizing ever since.

"I thank my lucky stars every day that you're not my boss too."

She slapped him with a stocking that she grabbed from a box. "You do not." Like her, Noah had made a big change this past year and moved to California to work for Riley Holdings, the company that owned the inn. Jackson hired him as their new commercial project manager because, in his words, "there were big plans on the horizon."

Noah pulled a large velvety box from a bag. Trace held her breath watching him open it. When he did, he plucked a candy cane out of it, one of many. "Don't give me that look. These are fake."

"They'd better be." A pulse of disappointment quickly changed to a smile as she watched him put fake candy canes on the branches of the tree. She remembered how distraught he looked after he'd discovered the tree that he had slept next to all night was virtually *alive* with insects, hungry, crawling insects.

"Don't mention those ants." He wore an expression of incredulity. "I can see it on your face!"

Trace laughed. "You have to admit it was hilarious."

"I would never admit that."

Thomas peeked his head in through the doorway and whistled. "You need something, Thomas?" Trace asked. What's with all the interruptions tonight? She was doing this off the clock, out of the goodness of her heart ...

Oh, who was she kidding?

Truth was, Trace had watched "It's a Wonderful Life" right after Thanksgiving again this year and the old movie had given her all the feels for the season. Nostalgia made her want to trim the tree with Noah again—without all the drama between them, of course. Oh, and those ants. Didn't want to see those again, either.

"Just saw the light on and thought I'd check to make sure everything is okay," he said. "Hey, cool, are those candy canes?" He started to approach when Trace and Noah simultaneously turned.

"They're fake!" they said in unison.

Thomas skidded to a stop. "Okay. Whoa. That's cool."

Once he'd left, Trace said, "Guess we'd better hurry up and finish or the entire staff will burst through the doors."

He was grinning at her now. "And we wouldn't want that now, would we?"

"Are you feeling okay? You're acting strange." Trace reached up and touched Noah's forehead with the back of her hand. "Nope. Cool as a cuke."

As she pulled her hand away, Noah took hold of it. He grinned and she quirked a smile in response. "What?"

"I've been wanting to ask you what you were doing for New Year's."

She shrugged. "I was thinking of making a pot of chili. Maybe watch the ball drop in New York and be done with it."

"Wow. That's ... a bold plan."

She laughed and brushed a gaze over his handsome face. "What do you suggest then?"

His grin broadened. "Well, since you asked." He kept her hand in his, his eyes on hers, and slowly knelt on the chapel floor. Noah tipped his chin up, eyes dancing now, and opened a small velvet box to reveal a dazzling diamond ring. "I say we get married."

She took in a quick uptick of breath.

"Marry me, Trace? On New Year's Eve? I don't want to spend another year without you as my wife."

Long before she met her dreamboat, she hoped for a moment like this. But she had not counted on the rush of emotion, the gratefulness of heart, and the sheer, unrelenting love that would whirl and dance its way through her at having the man she adored propose.

Everything was ... right. She froze, wanting to take it all in, afraid to close her eyes should it all fade away. But Noah raised a brow, asking her again with one determined look. She leaned forward, touching her nose to his, breathing him in. "Yes," she whispered. "I can't wait to marry you."

Noah kissed her tenderly and slowly rose as she gave out a little squeal. He slid the glistening ring onto her finger. "It's perfect! I love it!" Then she wrapped her arms around Noah's neck, squeezing him tight as a commotion came from outside.

"Did she say yes?" Hope was poking her head into the chapel, laughter and tittering flowing through the open doorway.

The door flung open and hit the wall. "Of course, she did!" Dinah shouted.

Hope wheeled her in. "I was just asking first!"

Noah threw back his head, laughing to the rafters. "Amen. Yes, she said yes!" Then with one big arc of his arm, he waved in a crew that had been, apparently, waiting with bated breath outside the chapel doors.

"About time," Dinah told Noah. Agatha was sitting on her lap, her collar tinkling. In a flash, Trace scooped her up and gave her mother a questioning look. "Said she wanted to be here with bells on."

"She made me do it," Hope said, wagging her head and smiling. "Congratulations, you two."

Behind them, Meg, Liddy, Priscilla, and Sophia streamed inside, encircling Trace while oohing and aahing over her ring.

"It's gorgeous!" Liddy called out.

"Stunning," Meg said.

"A perfect couple," Sophia murmured.

"A blessing!" Priscilla exclaimed.

To think Trace might have left all this behind a year

ago, when life looked so bleak from her side of the desk. Now all she could do was look around in wonder. Amid the celebration, Noah caught her eye and mouthed, *Merry Christmas, my love.*

Trace blew him a kiss, knowing without a doubt, there was nowhere else in the world she would rather be.

Acknowledgments

Thank you for reading this fifth installment of the Sea Glass Inn novels. Though I hadn't originally planned a fifth book, I couldn't forget the inn's long-suffering concierge, Trace. I'm so happy to give you her story, especially at Christmastime.

Thank you, Denise Harmer, for editing this book; Diana Lesire Brandmeyer and Stacy Holly for beta reading; and several long-time readers for your invaluable feedback.

Thank you also to my family—Dan, Matt, Angie, Emma, and my mom, Elaine—for always listening while I talk about what I'm working on, even when I'm a little stressed.

Most of all, thank you, readers, for coming along on the Sea Glass Inn journey with me! If you enjoyed *A Sea Glass Christmas,* please consider reviewing it on your favorite retail site and my website: JulieCarobini.com

Merry Christmas!

*J*ULIE

About the Author

JULIE CAROBINI writes inspirational beach romances. She is the author of 22+ books and is known for spunky heroines, charming heroes, quirky friends, and the secrets they keep. Her bestselling titles include *Walking on Sea Glass, Runaway Tide, Finding Stardust, Reunion in Saltwater Beach,* and more. Julie has received awards for writing and editing from The National League of American Pen Women and ACFW, and she is a double finalist for the ACFW Carol Award. She is the mother of three grown kids and lives on the California coast with her husband, Dan, and their rescue pup, Dancer.

Please visit her at
www.juliecarobini.com

Made in the USA
Las Vegas, NV
22 June 2023